THE WITCH WHO SAVED THE BAY

PIXIE POINT BAY BOOK 6

EMMA BELMONT

EMMA ONLINE

Emma loves hearing from her readers!

You can contact her at the links below.

Website: emmabelmont.com

Newsletter: emmabelmont.com/newsletter

Thanks!

Maris Seaver lifted her sign as high as she could. "Go away, not this bay!" she chanted, along with the rest of the crowd. "Go away, not this bay!"

Although the weather at the Pixie Point Bay Pier was as clear and temperate as ever, the mood of the protestors was decidedly foul. No fishermen dropped their lines into the pristine waters, and no one was perusing the catch of the day. Instead the long wharf was filled with the townspeople of Pixie Point Bay. As Maris started her second loop, she neared the reason for the protest: the two representatives of North American Petroleum.

The oil company had long made known

its desire to place an oil derrick in the bay. Maris could remember Aunt Glenda and Cookie talking about it at mealtime when she was a child. It seemed inconceivable to her that anyone would want to mar the beauty of such a picturesque scene. But it wasn't the drilling platform itself that had bothered Glenda, it was the possibility of an oil spill.

Imagine all the marine life gone, she'd said. *If it goes, we go.*

Her somber and worried tone had stuck with Maris all these years because, in the end, her aunt had been right. The longer that Maris lived here, the more she understood just how intertwined their lives were with the bay: from the fresh seafood for which the area was known, to the fishing economy, not to mention the tourism and visiting ships. Without all those boats, would there even be reason for a lighthouse?

Even if there's never a spill, Cookie had said, *it'd be ugly. Can you imagine waking up to that every morning in your backyard?*

The longtime chef of the B&B had nailed it. Maris couldn't imagine it—or wouldn't.

"Please everyone," Audrey Graisser said

through her megaphone. "Please, just let us have our say. This is a discussion, not a war."

In her mid-twenties, Audrey carried herself well. She wore her coppery red hair long, and her bright blue eyes always seemed to smile. She was dressed in a well-fitting gray business suit with a short skirt that showed off her pretty legs and figure. Though she seemed young for such a weighty job, Maris guessed she hadn't been picked for her vast experience. Her upbeat attitude and fresh face were completely winning. Despite understanding how cynical NAP had been when choosing her as a representative, Maris couldn't help but like her.

Though Audrey's companion was twice her age, he was equally charming. Joseph Toler, Esq., was no doubt on hand to make sure everything was done in compliance with regulations. He seemed to be able to recite them chapter and verse. His brunette hair was trimmed short and graying only at the sideburns. He smiled as much as Audrey, even surrounded by protestors, though his sea green eyes were alert. Like her, he was in business attire, but casual and without a tie.

He waved a hand above his head. "Please

everyone," he shouted, "we'd just like to report on the EIR."

The environmental impact report, Maris thought. Everyone in town now knew what EIR meant. Audrey and Joseph had been here for a few days already, canvasing the businesses door-to-door, and trying to drum up support. Judging by today's rally, they'd had little success.

"Pipe down," a familiar voice called out. *"Pipe down."*

Maris turned to see Slick standing on top of a wooden fish crate. The salty old seaman was waving his yellow slicker's hat. Despite the circumstances, she had to smile. Slick was a fixture on the pier. Day in and day out for decades, he kept the town supplied with the freshest and most varied seafood in this part of the world. As far as Maris was concerned, his long gray beard and leathery face only added to his charm. He'd been involved with her aunt, and now the two of them looked out for one another.

All around her his call for quiet was echoed. A few people murmured his name. When it came to the pier and the bay, Slick's word carried a lot of weight. As the chanting subsided, he said, "Let's not start a mutiny before the ship has set sail." Maris had to smirk.

He stepped down from the crate and held out a hand to Audrey, helping her to step up and take his place.

"Thank you, Captain Duff," she said, no longer using the megaphone. She handed it to Joseph. "And thank you all for being here." She smiled at many of the individuals she'd already met, including Maris. Both of the NAP representatives were staying at her B&B. "As many of you know, North American Petroleum is committed to the health and beauty of the bay."

Next to Maris, Howard Scry snorted, and she nodded her agreement to him. Owner of the Main Street Market, Howard bore an uncanny resemblance to Albert Einstein, only reinforced by the fact that he was a retired physics professor. "Beauty of the bay," he muttered, his white mustache twitching from side to side. "In a pig's eye."

Audrey breezily ignored the other similar rumblings from the crowd. "To that end, we have completed *two* independent EIRs." She waved a sheaf of papers in the air. "Copies of these are available right now." She indicated Joseph who began circulating through the crowd to hand them out. "Each of these companies has completed months of research and independently reported that any impact on the ecosystem of Pixie Point Bay would be nil."

Maris took a copy of the reports from Joseph as he passed by, as did Howard.

"Only if absolutely nothing went wrong," said Ryan Quigg. The young red head of Irish descent was not only the owner of the town's tackle shop, he was an avid fisherman. He was at the pier every morning. "What's the impact when there's a spill?"

"Yeah," someone else said. "What happens then?"

Audrey nodded. "I hear you. A spill would be a catastrophe. No doubt." She raised her voice a notch. "But let me remind you of North American Petroleum's track record." She made a circle with her finger and thumb. "Zero accidents." She paused for a moment. "Let me say that again. Zero. None. We're the company—and the only company I might add—with a perfect track record."

Though there were some shaking heads, no one contradicted her.

"It will be a complete and utter blight on the bay," Etienne Fournier said in his French accent. "Who is going to sit at my restaurant and look at such a monstrosity?" He waved his hand across the bay. "'And here is your wonderful view of metal.'" He shook his head. "No. I think not."

"And that is my second piece of good news today," Audrey said, looking at him. "North American Petroleum has decided to use a drillship, not an oil rig." Her smile was absolutely radiant. "You're not going to lose your wonderful view, Mr. Fournier. Your diners will simply see yet another ship in the bay."

Though Maris had never heard of a drillship, it didn't change the fact that liquid petroleum was going to be pumped from the bottom of the bay up to a waiting tanker. A massive industrial ship was a far cry from the luxury yachts and quaint sailboats that typically plied the waters. Nor did a perfect track record guarantee there wouldn't be an accident.

"And what about these documents?" a

woman's voice said.

She was moving through the crowd, her hand high in the air with her own set of papers. All the townspeople recognized her as well. Like the NAP representatives, Julia Mendes had arrived early, and was also staying at the B&B. It'd made for a tense few days, but everyone had done their best to be civil—mostly by avoiding one another.

"Company emails," she said, as everyone parted for her. Someone patted her on the back. "Internal communication that makes it clear that the so-called 'independent' EIRs are anything but."

The petite brunette made her way to the front. Older than Audrey, Julia was still a young woman, thirty at most. It was due to her hard work that today's rally had been organized. She'd made the flyers and the signs, and had held several small meetings around Pixie Point Bay to clearly outline their goals and strategies. She was an environmental activist with an already impressive list of accomplishments from hot spots around the globe. From the moment she'd arrived, she'd appeared as passionate about the bay as the residents.

She took up position directly in front of Audrey, turned to the crowd, and shook her papers angrily over her head. "Those EIRs were done by companies with direct ties to NAP." Without looking at Audrey, she jabbed a finger at her. "Direct *financial* ties." She glared at the faces in the crowd, and took a copy of the EIRs from someone nearby. "They paid for these findings, pure and simple." She hurled the papers to the planks of the wharf. "If those EIRs were printed on softer paper, they might actually be useful."

Someone in the back of the crowd laughed. Someone else said, "It's all rigged."

"You can read it for yourselves," Julia shouted, shaking her printed emails. "They think we're going to roll over. They think we're already in their pocket."

Joseph had returned to the front as well. Audrey turned a troubled look to him. Clearly this was supposed to be his area.

"Hearsay," he said simply. He spread his hands. "I've never heard of these emails until now, and I'm not going to debate them without even seeing them."

"Here!" Julia shouted, shoving them at him. "Go ahead. No one's stopping you."

"What do they say?" Ryan shouted.

"Read it," Howard yelled.

But as Audrey darted pleading looks at Joseph, he simply smiled, crossed his arms, and shook his head. "That's not how it works. There are ways to falsify these types of documents. Someone will have to prove to me that these are real before I look at them."

Now Audrey scowled at him. She climbed down off the fish crate, and said something into his ear. As the shouting rose louder, he shook his head again.

Now it was the environmental activist who climbed onto the box. "Go away, not this bay! Go away, not this bay!"

Soon the chanting was up to full force. Joseph dragged Audrey away and soon Maris lost them in the crowd. Meanwhile Julia thrust her fists up into the air. "Yes! Victory for Pixie Point Bay!"

But just as Maris was going to join in the chorus of hurrahs, she glanced across the bay. There, on the rocky promontory that jutted out into the water, the beam of her lighthouse flashed on and off.

"Uh oh," she said.

2

———

As Maris picked up another discarded flyer, she couldn't help but glance at the lighthouse again. It had flashed a warning, she was sure of it, and yet nothing had happened. The rally had been slow to break up with everyone celebrating along the entire length of the pier. Someone had brought a boom box, and dancing and singing had spontaneously broken out. But rather than join in, Maris had watched the crowd with a growing anxiety. The Old Girl never got it wrong.

"Thanks for your help, Maris," Julia said. "I really appreciate it."

The activist's olive skin gleamed not only from working hard under the hot sun, but with the energy of triumph as well. Her dark eyes sparkled, reflecting the bay that she'd worked so hard to protect. In her arms, she had gathered up all the signs that she and a handful of volunteers had made.

"It's the least I can do," Maris said. "Especially after everything you've done."

Not to mention, Maris thought, that Claribel had given her a warning. Not only did her magical lighthouse rescue sailors at sea, she also had an unerring way of spotting trouble on land. Something was going to happen in this direction. It was just a matter of time.

After picking up another flyer, Maris regarded the young woman. "So this is your work? Traveling around the world to help out places under threat?"

Julia nodded. "Places, species, water, forests, even ways of life. It's how I was raised. You might say I've been training since I could walk."

Ryan and Howard joined them, both carrying trash bags that were almost full. As Howard approached, he raised his hand to Julia, who gladly accepted his high five. "You did it," he said.

She shook her head. "We did it."

"They couldn't get away fast enough," Ryan said, who also gave her a high five, as well as Howard and Maris. "We've got them on the run."

Julia smiled at him. "That's for sure, but don't count them out." She stooped to pick up a sign from a bench they passed, heading back toward the beginning of the pier. The two men fell into step behind them. "They'll be back. NAP hasn't invested tons of money to drill for oil here, just to drop the whole thing because of our rally."

"They're never drilling for oil here," Ryan said. "Not as long as I'm here."

"Over my dead body," Howard said, with enough vehemence that Maris turned to look at him. He was glowering out at the water, unaware of her gaze.

"Careful what you ask for," Julia said, suddenly sober as well.

Maris frowned. It was as though her anxiety over the Old Girl's signal had spread to her companions.

As they passed, *Seas the Day*, Slick's fishing boat, he gave them a wave. "You took the wind out of their sails," he called out to Julia. "Carry on with the good work."

She grinned and waved back at him. "Thanks for your help, Captain Duff!"

Maris smiled and waved at the old fisherman too, as Ryan cupped a hand to his mouth and yelled, "May the catching be as good as the fishing!" He gave Slick a thumb's up, and the old seafarer gave him a wave.

As they approached the parking lot, Maris saw that the sheriff's SUV was one of the few vehicles remaining. For a moment she worried that perhaps he'd been summoned for some emergency. But from the way he leaned against the front bumper and sipped from a travel mug, there didn't seem to be any rush.

They came to Julia's rental first. "Here," she said, popping open the trunk. "Just put everything in here."

"Are you sure?" Maris said. "We can help you sort through everything."

"No worries," the young woman said, putting in the signs. "There'll be plenty of time later. They're going to have to regroup, and this won't be our last rally."

Maris laid the flyers in next to them.

"I'll get rid of these at the market," Howard said, taking Ryan's trash bag from him. "I've got a big dumpster out back."

"Thank you," Julia said. "That'd be great." She closed the trunk, and stood back to regard her three helpers. "You guys have been wonderful. We did good today."

"Good work, everybody," Howard said, smiling, seemingly back to his old self.

"Let me know if you need anything else," Ryan said.

"Will do," Julia said, and watched them go.

"I'll see you back at the B&B," Maris said to her.

"Sounds good," she said, grinning. "That wine and cheese is going to be good tonight."

As Maris watched her go, she tried to imagine the Wine Down. More than likely Julia would be in the mood for a bit of gloating. But equally as likely, the two NAP representatives would probably be in the mood for dinner out and to avoid the environmentalist altogether.

As Maris turned back to where she'd seen

the sheriff, he was approaching. "Hello, Mac," she said, smiling. "What brings you to the pier on this beautiful day?"

"Just ensuring the peace," he said, returning her smile. His gray eyes seemed lit from within as he gazed at her. As usual, his brown and khaki uniform was neatly pressed, and the star badge on his breast pocket gleamed a bright gold. "I've been here most of the morning."

"Oh!" she said, glancing around. "I didn't see you."

He smirked a little. "That's pretty much the point. I expected it to be peaceful, which it was. But I'm paid to be a pessimist, you might say." He paused for a moment. "'The past was bad, and the future hid, its good or ill untried, but the present hour, was in my power.'"

She laughed a little. "I see. Expect the best, and plan for the worst, even for Robert Burns."

He nodded. "That's it exactly. When you've been–"

"Sheriff!" someone yelled. Maris spun around to see Jill Maxwell running in their direction. The nurse practitioner from the Pixie Point Bay Medical Clinic was pointing behind her to the steps that led down to the sand. "Come quick," she gasped. "There's a body, under the pier."

3

———

Mac crouched down near the body, laying on its side. As Maris looked on, it was hard to make out what was going on in the deep shadows. Beyond them the high tide was rhythmically approaching and retreating, and the sound of the waves seemed amplified under the pier's massive columns and beams. Maris stood next to Jill, who gripped her arm.

"Did you see who it was?" Maris asked.

Jill nodded. "The woman from North American Petroleum. I don't know her name."

"What?" Maris whispered as she went still. "Audrey Graisser?"

"Right," Jill said. "That's her name. Audrey."

Claribel had been right. An icy shiver ran down Maris's spine. Deadly trouble had literally been brewing right under her feet.

But Audrey?

Maris could hardly believe it. As much as the town didn't want an oil derrick in the bay, no one would have wanted to see the likable young woman hurt, let alone dead. And yet, that's exactly what seemed to have happened. Maris glanced back in the direction of the lighthouse. The Old Girl had tried to tell her.

As Mac stood, he placed his phone back in its holder. Then he glanced around at the ground before coming back to where they waited. He exchanged a grim look with Maris before turning to Jill.

"I assume you touched the body," he said.

She let go of Maris's arm. "Yes. I immediately checked for a pulse."

"Anything else?" he asked.

The nurse shook her head. "No. It was apparent that she was...beyond help."

Maris looked at her, and then at Mac. Though she was fairly sure she didn't want to know the answer, she felt compelled to ask, "How did she die?"

The sheriff grimaced. "It looks like some sort of spear. It went right through her."

"Good grief," Maris gasped.

"It looks to me like she bled out," Jill said. "Quickly."

"That's what it looks like," Mac agreed. "Nevertheless I've called the coroner and forensics. They'll be here shortly." He regarded the nurse. "Did you see anyone in the vicinity?"

She shook her head again. "No. I came down here for a walk along the water before heading back to town. Everyone else had already left. As far as I could tell, I was alone."

He nodded. "And I was waiting in the parking lot, supposedly keeping the peace."

Maris heard the self-recrimination in his voice. She sympathized because she felt the same. They'd both been standing not one hundred yards away, and she'd even been warned.

"There was no reason to think anything was going on down here," Maris said. She glanced at the shadowed body. "She must not have had time to scream for help."

"Or the sound of the surf drowned it out," Jill said.

"Or she never saw it coming," Mac said. He looked at the ground in their vicinity. "The sand is too dry for footprints."

Maris saw a movement near the body. It was one of the rally flyers, rustled by the breeze. "Look," she said, pointing to it.

"I saw that," Mac said, looking at it. "There are a few of them in the vicinity. One in the water." He looked toward the parking lot. "But we'll wait for forensics to collect them."

"They might have drifted down from above," Jill suggested.

"It's possible," Mac said. "Or they could have been dropped by the murderer, or even the victim." He grimaced again. "We'll just have to wait and see."

For a moment the three of them only looked on in silence. Maris noted the muscles at Mac's jaw working. Then he sighed and reached into his pocket and brought out a business card.

"If there's anything you remember later," he said, handing it to Jill, "no matter how small or seemingly insignificant, please don't hesitate to let me know."

Jill took the card. "Sure. I doubt there'll be much, since you've seen what I've seen."

"Thanks," Mac said.

Jill looked at Maris. "I'm going to head back to the clinic." She smiled a little. "But thanks for...holding my hand."

"Any time," Maris said. "It's a bit of a shock, to be sure." Even to a medical professional, Maris thought. And even to me. Cold filled the pit of her stomach, and she was glad to be well back from the crime scene.

When Jill left, Mac turned back to the body and crossed his arms over his chest. "Right under my nose," he muttered.

Although she'd wanted to say that there was no way that either of them could have prevented the young woman's death, she wasn't so sure that was true.

"Under all of ours," she said grimly.

Mac glanced back at her, and then over her shoulder. "Here's the coroner."

Maris didn't bother to turn. Voight would likely not acknowledge her anyway. But as he passed them, followed by his assistant, he surprised her.

"Sherriff," he said without pausing or looking. "Ms. Seaver."

"Mr. Voight," Mac said.

"Good morning," Maris finally managed to say.

Of average build and height, the coroner appeared to be in his early fifties. His jet black hair was graying just a bit at the temples, but his high forehead was deeply wrinkled. The bright yellow of the word "CORONER" on the back of his black windbreaker glowed despite the shade of the pier. He came to an abrupt stop and signaled to his assistant to stand back. Apparently he'd seen the spear. As Mac had done, Voight looked at the ground around him. Seemingly satisfied, he moved carefully closer and crouched next to the body, in the same spot as Mac.

"Sheriff," said a woman's voice.

Maris turned to see the forensics crew. The older woman was in the lead, as usual. A bit on the heavy side with light brown eyes, Maris suspected that the blonde highlights she could see through the hairnet came from a bottle. Though she already wore the biohazard coverall, plastic goggles and gloves, her surgical mask dangled from her neck.

She eyed the coroner. "He really ought to

wait until we're done." Mac started to reply, but she waved him off. "Oh believe me, I've tried too."

Maris had never heard her speak so much—or perhaps had not heard her clearly. Only now did she realize that the woman had just the slightest hint of a Southern accent.

Mac must have seen Maris looking at her. "Maris Seaver," he said, "Lucile Trahan, Crime Scene Investigator."

"Nice to meet you," Maris said, not offering to shake her gloved hand.

The other woman nodded as well. "I recognize you from the B&B." She thought for a moment. "The murder of that gaming guy."

"Right," Maris said.

"Maris was here when the body was discovered," the sheriff said.

The woman turned to indicate her assistant. "Sefina Kealoha, my new Forensic Technician."

"Sefina," Maris said. The young woman already had her mask up, but it didn't hide her high cheekbones. Her dark, angular eyes glanced at the sheriff and Maris.

"Pleased to meet you," Sefina said.

Despite the coverall suit, Sefina was obviously petite, even shorter than Maris.

"Come on," Lucile said with a heavy sigh. "Let's get over there before they make a mess of my crime scene."

As Maris and Mac watched, the two teams worked around one another. But it was clear, even at a distance, that there was precious little evidence. The flyers were photographed in place, then bagged and labeled. But there was nothing else. As Mac had already noted, there weren't even any footprints.

It didn't take long for everyone to finish up. Voight and his assistant enlisted the aid of the investigators and Mac. A normal rolling stretcher wasn't possible on the sand. Instead they used what appeared to be a canvas stretcher, gripping the fabric loops all around the edge as handholds.

Nor did they use a body bag. The long metal spear wouldn't fit. Instead, the coroner draped a few sheets over the body. As Maris watched, they managed to get up the steps and over to the van. She opened the doors on the back and stepped aside. Gently, the group settled Audrey on the floor.

As they all climbed back out, Voight took off his latex gloves. "I'll be in touch," he said to Mac, before closing the doors on the van.

"Same here," said the lead investigator.

"Thanks," Mac said.

There'd been very little talk the entire time, and now Maris wondered if everyone might be thinking what she was: the people who'd most want to see a representative of North American Petroleum dead were the people of Pixie Point Bay.

As the two vehicles pulled away, Mac said, "Her colleague, Joseph Toler. I take it he's staying at your place?"

Maris nodded. "Yes, as is Julia Mendes."

Mac took out his keys. "I'll meet you there."

4

From the entrance to the driveway, Maris had seen that both Toler and Mendes were at the B&B since their cars were parked outside. As they came to the front door, Mac opened it for her.

"I'd like to speak with Toler first," he said, then closed the door behind her. "Ms. Graisser's next of kin need to be notified. NAP ought to have that information."

"Right," Maris said, recalling the phone conversation she'd had with Mac all those months ago when her aunt had died. The sound of a male voice came from the library, and it didn't sound like their handyman. "That must be him."

Joseph Toler was still wearing the casual suit and shirt he'd been wearing at the pier.

He was alone in the library and on his cell phone.

"It's not a matter of dueling EIRs," he said, pacing toward the window, his voice insistent and strained. He turned to walk in the opposite direction. "It's a matter of–" He came to an abrupt stop when he saw Mac and Maris in the doorway. "I'll call you back." He thumbed off the power.

"Mr. Toler," Mac said. "I'm Sheriff McKenna. I'd like to have a word with you."

The lawyer dropped his phone into his pants pocket. "Okay," he said, his tone neutral although a wary look crossed his face.

"Would you like to have a seat?" Mac asked.

"No," Joseph said. "I'd prefer to stand." He glanced at Maris, and then back to the sheriff. "What's this about?"

"I'm afraid I have some bad news," Mac said. "It's about Audrey Graisser."

The lawyer blinked, and his eyebrows rose. "Audrey?" Then he frowned. "What bad news?"

"I'm afraid she's died," the sheriff said plainly. "Her body was found on the beach, near the pier."

"*What?*" Joseph demanded. He shook his head. "Hold on. Audrey Graisser. My Audrey?"

"Yes," Mac said. "Your colleague."

There was silence for a few moments as Toler seemed to have trouble processing what Mac had said. "That's not possible. I just left her. I'm waiting for her to call." He shook his head again. "There's been some mistake."

Mac leveled his gaze at the lawyer. "I'm afraid there's been no mistake. I saw the body myself. Audrey Graisser is dead."

"But..." Toler looked at Maris. "But...how can that be?" He stared at Mac. "How did she die?"

"It appears that she was murdered," the sheriff said.

Joseph cocked his head back, his eyes huge. "What?" But as the information sank in, his face began to turn red. "How?" he said loudly. "What happened?"

"I'm waiting for reports from the coroner and forensics team," Mac said truthfully, though it was clear what had killed the poor girl.

"Waiting?" Toler yelled. "Waiting? What are you doing about it?"

"Joseph," Maris said, "maybe you'd like a glass of water."

"What I'd like is to know what in the hell you're doing about this?" he yelled at Mac, who stood his ground but didn't retort. The lawyer threw his hands in the air and stalked back to the window. "I can't believe this. Audrey is dead?" He whirled back around and jabbed a finger at Mac. "You were supposed to prevent that. You were supposed to be there and make sure we didn't get hurt."

"I was there," the sheriff replied, his voice rising as well, "to protect everyone, not just you two. The rally ended peacefully and–"

"Is that what you call peacefully?" Toler demanded, the red of his face deepening. He put his hand to his forehead and stared at the ground. "I can't believe this is happening."

"Mr. Toler," the sheriff said, "I've got some questions for you."

"Not as many as I have for you," the lawyer shot back, dropping his hand. "You better believe I'm going to make my own investigation."

"You have that right," Mac said. "But you

do not have the right to impede mine. You can answer my questions here, or you can answer them in my office." Mac took a notepad from his breast pocket.

Though Toler didn't seem any more calm, he'd apparently understood the sheriff's meaning. "Ask," he said curtly.

"At the end of the rally," Mac said, "you left with Ms. Graisser. When was the last time you saw her?"

"In the SUV," he said. "We had to take cover there after you let the rally get out of control."

Mac ignored the accusation. "The SUV that's parked outside?"

"Yes," the lawyer said.

The sheriff made a note. "So you drove here without her?"

The lawyer sighed. "Obviously. She wanted to stay and liaise one-on-one. I told her it was a bad idea. The crowd had grown ugly."

Though Maris didn't contradict him, that wasn't how she'd seen it. But maybe if you were standing in the midst of a chanting crowd, everyone focused on you, it felt different.

"So she got out of the SUV?" Mac asked.

"Yes," Toler confirmed. "She got out of the SUV, and I came back here. That was the last time I saw her."

"And what time was that?" the sheriff said.

The lawyer checked his watch. "Two hours ago. She was going to call and we were going to catch an early dinner."

Mac jotted down the information. "Did she say who in particular she was going to see?"

"No one in particular," he said, and paused. "But why don't you ask that loud-mouthed fisherman, the young one, or his buddy, Einstein?"

Maris frowned, but Mac only said, "I'll be speaking with everyone, Mr. Toler. For now, maybe you could tell me how long you've known Audrey."

The lawyer shook his head. "I don't know her at all. We only met when we arrived here. I'm one of many legal counsels for the company. I've never worked with her before."

"Did she mention anyone with whom she was at odds? Any enemies?"

The lawyer smirked. "Enemies," he

scoffed. "Hardly. That's exactly why NAP hires someone like her."

"Because she's so likable," Maris agreed.

"If you're searching for culprits," Toler yelled, "why don't you start in town?" Then he looked up at the ceiling. "Or with that shrill activist upstairs. If you want to find someone who'd want to see her dead, I'd suggest you start there."

"One final question, Mr. Toller," the sheriff said. "Do you have the contact information for her supervisor at NAP?"

The lawyer blinked at him. "I think so. I mean, I can dig it up. Why?"

"I'll need her emergency contact information so that her next of kin can be notified."

Toler suddenly deflated. "Oh," he said. "I see. Yes."

Mac took out a business card. "When you get it, you can call or text." He handed it to the lawyer, who glared down at it. The lawyer's shoulders suddenly sagged.

"She was so young," he muttered.

"Yes," the sheriff said, his voice tight. "She was." As he tucked his notepad away, he said. "Plan to stay in town for at least the next few days. I'll have the coroner and forensics reports by then."

Toler was instantly angry again. "I'll be in your face until the murderer is brought to justice, however long that takes."

As Maris escorted Mac upstairs, she said, "Julia's room is at the end." But she needn't have. Julia Mendes was waiting for them.

With a tissue already to her nose, and her eyes watery and red, she was shaking. "Audrey?" she gasped. "Audrey is...dead?"

Of course she must have heard Joseph screaming on the first floor.

Mac nodded, his face grim. "I'm afraid so. Yes."

Julia shook her head. "No," she whispered. "No, no, no." She staggered a bit and Maris quickly moved forward at the same time as Mac. They each took an elbow.

"This way," Maris said, as the three of them managed to get through the door of her bedroom and over to the bed. Julia sat down hard.

Maris went back into the hallway, and fetched a glass of water from the bathroom. By the time she brought it back, Mac was supporting the young woman with a hand on her shoulder.

"Take a sip," Maris told her.

She quickly took the glass in shaking hands and managed to spill as much on her jeans as she drank. "Thank you," she gasped.

Over the top of her head, Maris exchanged a look with Mac. This wasn't the reaction of a killer.

"I..." she began, then paused to gulp some air. "I had nothing to do with...whatever happened to her." She looked up at the sheriff, her eyes streaming tears. "I had nothing against her. She was doing her job. I was doing mine." Then her face screwed up. "The last thing on earth I'd do is make it personal, let alone physical." She looked up at Maris. "You have to believe me."

Maris looked into her eyes. "We're going to get to the truth," she assured her. "You can count on it."

Mac took the moment to stand back. "When was the last time you saw her?"

Julia wiped her eyes. "When they left the pier. After that, I never saw her again." Maris brought the box of tissues from the dresser and set it on the bed. Julia immediately took a couple. "Thanks."

"Where were you after the rally?" Mac said, taking out his notepad.

"We..." she said and glanced at Maris. "Ryan, Howard, and Maris helped me pick up trash."

Mac gazed at Maris, who nodded, then directed his attention back to Julia. "How long did that take?"

Julia took a ragged, deep breath and shrugged. "I don't know. Maybe an hour?"

Maris nodded again. "I'd say that's about right. The four of us were on the pier picking up the signs and flyers, along with some soda cans and water bottles."

"Were you always within sight of one another?" the sheriff asked.

Maris had to think back on it, but finally shook her head. "I don't think so."

"I don't think so either," Julia said. "We

kind of split up to cover as much ground as possible."

Which meant, Maris thought, that none of them had an alibi.

Mac made a note. "And when you were done with the cleanup, what happened then?"

"We put the signs and flyers in the trunk of the car," Julia said, dabbing her eyes again. "Howard took the trash bags to throw away at his market. Then I came here." She glanced at the bedroom door. "No one else was here, so I came straight up to check my email."

"So, no one saw you arrive?" he asked, as he made another note.

"No," Julia said. "At least I didn't see anyone."

"All right," the sheriff said, closing the notepad. He tucked it back into his breast pocket. "The last thing I'd like to do right now," he said, taking out a plastic bag from his pants pocket, "is to take your fingerprints."

"My fingerprints?" the young woman said, looking alarmed.

"It's standard procedure," Maris said. "Mine are already on file."

"That's right on both counts," Mac said. "It really is just a formality." He indicated the dresser. "If you'll step over here, it'll only take a moment."

Though she still seemed a bit shaky, Julia stood at the dresser in silence as Mac took each print. But by the time he produced the cleaning towelette and a business card, the young woman's face had gone decidedly pale.

"Maybe you should have a seat," Maris said.

But Julia quickly shook her head. "I think I'm going to be sick."

She staggered to the bathroom and slammed the door behind her. As Mac put away the fingerprint card and pad, they could clearly hear that Julia was indeed sick. He laid the card and towelette on the nightstand, before he and Maris went back downstairs.

"I'll check on her in a bit," Maris said quietly.

Joseph was pacing outside, beyond Cookie's garden, still on the phone. It was already late afternoon, the sun beginning its descent to the sea. A thin layer of clouds at the horizon were gleaming a pale pink that Maris knew would soon turn violet.

Only now did she realize she'd missed lunch. Somehow her appetite had gone. But hungry or not, the setting sun signaled that it was time to prepare the evening's wine and cheese.

As she and Mac moved toward the front of the house, Maris said, "Looks like it's time to get the cheeseboard started."

He regarded her as they reached the front door. "You really think that Toler or Mendes is going to be in the mood?"

"Oh no," Maris said, with a little smile. "I sincerely doubt it. No, we have two other guests here this week. They might be back soon, so I'll need to get ready." She glanced up at the ceiling. "Honestly, having additional people has helped to ease the tension here. Everyone has been on good behavior."

Mac grimaced. "Until today."

Maris's smile fell. "Right," she muttered. "Until today."

Mac opened the door. "After I've been in touch with Ms. Graisser's next of kin, I'll pack up her belongings. If you could just lock her room until then, I'd appreciate it."

"Sure thing," Maris said.

"Thanks for all your help, as usual, Maris. I'll be in touch when I know more."

"Thanks, Mac."

When he turned to go, she gently closed the door behind him. Those coroner and forensics reports couldn't come soon enough.

6

In the kitchen, Maris went to the giant steel refrigerator and took a look at the day's cheese assortment. As she was pondering their possibilities, a tiny, tinny harmonica like meow called her attention to the floor.

"Mojo," she said, to her little but pudgy black cat. "Your hearing is as good as ever." His big orange eyes gazed up at her, and she had to smile. No matter what happened during the day, his presence always managed to comfort her. Inquisitive and affectionate, he never changed. "What do you say to a snack?" In answer, he gave an even louder meow. Named after harmonica player George "Mojo" Buford, he sounded more like his namesake than ever. Maris had to chuckle. "Never turn down a snack. Words to live by."

She removed a couple of cheeses from the refrigerator, as well as his container of smoked salmon, and took them to the counter. Rather than follow her, he bounced lightly across the tile floor to wait by his bowl. She used a serving spoon to dish up a nice portion of the fish, and took it to the bowl. His glittering eyes followed her every move and no sooner had the fish landed in his dish, he lunged forward, burying his nose.

"Um, you're welcome," Maris said.

At least someone had a good appetite.

Hopefully the fact that she'd missed lunch would work in her favor at the usual morning weigh-in. It was always the last bunch of pounds that were the slowest to come off. But her clothes were definitely feeling more comfortable, and she had started to see the good results in the mirror.

As she washed her hands and took the cheeseboard and cheeses to the dining room's sideboard, she turned her thoughts to what wines would compliment them. Often hosts would choose the wine first. Typically it was the more expensive component. But to

Maris it didn't matter where you started, as long as you ended up pleasing your guests.

As she sliced the aged Gouda—fresh from the dairy in Cheeseman Village—she decided its nutty flavor would stand up well to the full body of a cabernet. The fruity Gruyere, however, would go very nicely with a Chardonnay. From the pantry she brought out some water crackers, dates, and dried cherries. As a special treat, mostly for herself, she used her chocolate superpower to easily sniff out the Belgian dark chocolate she'd been saving.

Back in the dining room, she had just finished the last touches on the cheeseboard when the door to the back porch opened. A few seconds later, Lydia Urbonas joined her.

"Lydia," Maris said, smiling. "Your timing is impeccable. I'm just about to open the wine. Chardonnay or Cabernet for you?"

The young brunette flashed her bright smile. "Oh, Cabernet please. Thank you."

Maris judged Lydia's age to be somewhere in her early thirties. Of average height and weight, she was incredibly fit—not chunky, but not a waif either. If there was a single word that Maris would pick to describe her, it would be solid. She wore a fitted t-shirt and shorts, and carried a towel, which she set on a chair.

Maris brought out a glass for red wine to the dining table and poured, while Lydia took a small plate and began to serve herself at the sideboard. "I'll leave your wine here."

"Thank you," Lydia said.

Maris was just considering what she would have, when the front door opened. The sound of footsteps was followed by Ralph Karsten coming through the dining room entrance.

"Greetings, one and all," he said, grinning.

Though Maris guessed that the young man would once have had dark hair to match his eyes, he was completely bald. But the lack of hair did nothing to diminish his appeal. Outgoing and energetic, he had the build of a gymnast.

"I see I'm just in time," he said, moving directly to the sideboard. He examined both wines. "Classics." He eyed what Lydia was having, and then poured himself a Cabernet as well. "I've been looking forward to this all day." Then he took a plate. "What have you two been up to?"

Maris hesitated, hoping that Lydia would take the lead, which she did.

"I kayaked the bay today," she said. That would explain her attire and the fact that she'd come in from the back, the location of the dock. "It was lovely, and the kayaks are in excellent repair."

The previous evening, neither Julia nor Joseph or Audrey had come down for wine. It had just been the three of them, as it was tonight. Maris had learned that Lydia was a traveling salesman and a fitness buff. She sold all manner of water sports equipment. Ralph, on the other hand, was probably her ideal customer. He was a travel blogger and photographer, with a penchant for adventure and the outdoors.

"Really?" he said. "I haven't been on the bay yet."

"Well what are you waiting for?" Lydia chided.

He smiled. "Just getting my bearings." He took a bite of the Gouda that he paired with the water cracker and a date. "Ooh, that is good."

Maris smiled. "I'm glad you're enjoying it."

Lydia turned to her. "Have you ever considered adding paddleboards to your kayaks?"

"Paddleboards?" Maris said, taking some chocolate to go with her Chardonnay. "Are those the things that kids use for surfing?"

Lydia grinned at her. "You're thinking of boogie boards." She set down her wine and pantomimed a canoe-rowing action. "You stand on the board and use a paddle."

"Goodness," Maris said, putting some cheese and dried cherries on her plate. "Like a gondolier."

"Oh my god," Ralph said, lifting his wine glass to her. "I can't believe you said that. I've actually paddleboarded in Venice."

Lydia almost choked on her wine. "You what?"

"Lydia," he said, beaming at her. "Believe me when I tell you that I am living the dream. I make a living from my travel blog. I go where I want, when I want, and do as I please. And yes, I've paddleboarded the canals in Venice."

"How do you make a living from a blog?" she asked.

"I sell advertising space, get paid for endorsements, give inside tips and product discounts to my newsletter subscribers, if they're part of the inner circle. Some destinations will actually pay me to visit." He took a sip of his wine. "I haven't had to buy equipment in years. Companies just send it to me."

"Wow," both she and Maris said.

"That's amazing," Lydia said.

"You travel as well," he said to her.

"Kind of," she said, shrugging and looking at the ground. "I rep paddleboards and canoes up and down the coast." But then she grinned. "But I adore my job. I love being able to introduce people to the things that really get me fired up: fitness and water sports."

He smiled back at her. "Well there you go. You're living the dream too."

Lydia turned to Maris, as she filled up her plate again. "Speaking of which, would you like to try the paddleboard? I'd be glad to show you. It's a completely different view of the bay than you'd get in a kayak."

As Maris took more chocolate and placed it on top of a slice of cheese, she thought about it. "They sound pretty low maintenance." Unfortunately, Maris had never particularly excelled at sports—or coordination for that matter. Then she gazed down at all the calories on her plate, before looking up at Lydia. "It's probably something I should look into for my guests. "

"Super easy to take care of," the younger woman said. "You've got that right." She looked at the travel blogger. "And you're invited, Ralph. Just as long as you don't leave us in your wake."

He laughed, a warm and pleasant sound. "No, no. I'm not into speed. I'm in it for the experience." He looked out the bay window to the last rays of the setting sun. "And after today's news, I'll bet we have the bay all to ourselves."

Lydia was finishing her first glass of wine, and got up for a refill. "What news is that?"

"You didn't hear?" he asked, taking a piece of the Gruyere. "That oil company representative was killed over at the rally today."

Lydia was coming back with her new glass of wine, but stopped. "Here? In Pixie Point Bay?"

He nodded. "At the pier. It's all over the internet."

Lydia turned a shocked look to Maris. "Did you know about it?"

For a moment, she considered saying no. It'd been such a pleasant and distracting evening. But she could hardly lie. "I'm afraid so. In fact, the victim, Audrey Graisser, was a guest here."

"Oh no," Ralph said. "Here?"

Maris had that familiar sinking feeling in her stomach. "Yes, with her colleague."

"Well," he said, looking at Maris and then Lydia. "It looks like we're in the thick of it." He regarded Maris. "I'll be blogging about it tonight. I don't suppose there's any light you can shed?"

She shook her head. "I'm afraid not," she lied. She went to the sideboard and grabbed another handful of chocolate. "We'll just have to wait and see what the authorities say."

"Well they'd better hurry," Ralph said. "The internet trolls have already come out, and the blame for her death is landing with the town."

"What?" Maris said, incredulous. "The

investigation's barely started."

Ralph had to laugh. "Like that's going to stop anyone from voicing their 'humble opinions' and casting accusations." Then he gave Lydia and Maris a quick look. "But I don't get into the politics. I base my blog on what's actually happening, right up to the minute sometimes. I'm as even handed as I can be."

Maris nodded. "I'm sure. Of course. But it's a little troubling to hear about the reaction on the internet."

He grimaced. "Welcome to my world."

"Well, I haven't heard a thing about it," Lydia said. "I was on the water all day."

As Ralph filled her in over wine, Maris took a seat. Pixie Point Bay depended on tourism in order to thrive. But more than that, she had gotten to know most of the people here—and they were good. Besides, if one of the magic folk had really wanted to see someone dead, it'd have been done a great deal more subtly than a spear.

She glanced out the window to the darkening waters. Now more than ever, she had to get to the bottom of this. She absently popped another piece of chocolate in her mouth.

7

———

As the first rays of the morning sun began to filter into Maris's bedroom, she was just finishing in the bathroom. Done with brushing out her thick, strawberry blonde hair, all that was left was the drying. She picked up her shiny new red dryer, with its sleek, flat nozzle. When she'd trotted the globe for her job, she'd been relegated to a compact model or whatever the hotel had installed. This one was rated with twice the power of her old one and came with fancy attachments, including one that looked like a giant shower head.

She plugged it in and thumbed on the switch. The dryer roared to life—and promptly died, taking with it the lights in the bathroom and the lamp in the bedroom.

Still lying on the bed, Mojo meowed plaintively.

She looked over at him, frowning. "Agreed," she muttered.

Although she flicked the hair dryer off, the lights in the bathroom remained dark, and nothing in the bedroom seemed to be on. She went to the nightstand. Her phone wasn't charging.

Hair still wet, she paused at the bed to give Mojo a scratch behind the ears. "It's probably a breaker."

But just to be sure, she opened the bedroom door and went into the hallway. She turned on the light there without a problem, and she could hear Cookie in the kitchen. The rest of the house seemed fine. As Mojo trotted past her toward the kitchen, she turned and went back to the desk and picked up the phone. Using it like a flashlight, she went into the utility room, past the basement door, and directly to the breaker panel. She opened the gray metal door. Although nothing was labelled, one breaker in particular was out of line with the rest.

"Gotcha," she said, reaching for it. Although she shoved it back into place, it wouldn't stick. It immediately flipped back to the first position. She frowned at it, clicking it over again. Three more attempts resulted in the same thing.

Could something else be making it trip?

She went back into the bathroom and unplugged the hair dryer, but back in the utility room, the breaker still wouldn't stay on. Down to her last and least favorite resort, she unplugged everything in the bedroom as well, wondering if perhaps she'd damaged one of the appliances with an electrical spike. Huffing and puffing after having to crawl under the desk as well as move the nightstand, she tried the breaker again.

Nothing.

"Great," she muttered.

Not only would she need to have Bear take a look at the breaker box, her hair was a mess, and her new time-saving hair dryer had cost her at least half an hour. She needed to stop messing around and help with breakfast.

8

Maris hurried to the kitchen to find that Ruth "Cookie" Calderon had almost finished. Despite being late—or maybe because of it—Cookie's smile seemed extra wide. She turned from the stove to look over her shoulder at Maris.

"Good morning," she said. Diminutive and in her early seventies, Cookie's straight black hair was more silver than black these days, but her dark eyes shone with the light of someone decades younger. She also had an energy that a middle-aged Maris could barely keep up with.

"Good morning," Maris replied. "Sorry I'm late."

Cookie's eyes went to her hair, which

Maris tried to push back into place. But the older woman made no comment on it. "That's a pretty skirt," she said.

Like her Aunt Glenda, who she resembled, Maris preferred skirts to slacks, and solids to patterns. Today her skirt fell just below the knee, aqua with a dark blue border. Her long-sleeved blouse was white, but with matching blue pin-stripes.

"Thanks," she said. "My hair dryer tripped a breaker and I couldn't get it to come back on."

"Oh?" the chef said, glancing in that direction before returning her attention to the stove. "A job for Bear?"

"I think so," Maris answered. She crossed the large kitchen and looked over the chef's shoulder. "I thought I smelled cinnamon. Oh, those look wonderful."

The last batch of cinnamon French toast was in the pan. In the warming trays to the side, the thick sliced and golden brown bread was sprinkled with both cinnamon and powdered sugar. But at the sight of the other tray, Maris clasped her hands together.

"Mini omelets?" She grinned and glanced

back at Cookie. "You know these are my favorite, right?"

Cookie cast a long sideways glance at her. "Uh huh," she said slowly.

Though the diminutive chef might doubt her sincerity, it was true. Her interpretation of the word 'favorite' might be a bit loose, but Maris had simply never met one of Cookie's specialties that she didn't positively adore.

The mini omelets looked done to perfection, and positively full of fresh ingredients that Maris recognized: a triple cream Brie from Cheeseman Village and sautéed mushrooms, sprinkled with chives and fresh ground pepper. Homemade tater tots finished off the offerings, and a generous plate of sliced heirloom tomatoes was also ready.

Maris quickly scanned the counters. "Can I squeeze the orange juice?"

Cookie nodded. "That would be lovely." She used her spatula to point to the butcher block. "And I steeped some tea for you while I made my own."

It'd taken months, but Cookie had finally weaned her away from her jolt of morning caffeine. Although, truth be told, she still sometimes snuck an afternoon cup for a pick-me-up.

"Thank you," Maris said, bringing it to the counter and taking a sip. "Mmm. From the garden?"

Cookie nodded. "Chamomile, mint, and lemon verbena."

"Wonderful," Maris said, setting it down, and grabbing a few oranges.

"How was the rally yesterday?" Cookie asked. "It must have lasted longer than planned."

Maris paused. "Um, not exactly."

At the tone in her voice, the chef looked over. "What?"

As Maris recounted the grim details of Audrey's death, Cookie's face registered the shock. "That beautiful girl," she whispered. "I'm so sorry to hear this."

For a few moments they stood in silence, until Maris said, "Not that her death isn't tragic enough, but it seems that the townsfolk of Pixie Point Bay are getting the blame."

"Us?" Cookie said, but then she cast her glance toward the window, in the direction of the town. She heaved a heavy sigh. "I suppose it's to be expected." She looked at the warming trays. "Well, let's get a move on. The living need to eat."

Maris helped the chef move everything to the dining room sideboard, followed by fresh coffee in the vacuum carafe and orange juice in the pretty decanter. She had just finished checking the hot water dispenser when Joseph came down the stairs and into the dining room.

"Good morning," Maris said, smiling.

His grim expression was complemented by his tousled hair and blood-shot eyes. He looked like he hadn't slept. "Not particularly."

Maris knew better than to reply. If anyone blamed the townsfolk more, Maris couldn't imagine who it would be. After his outburst with Mac yesterday, his greeting was under-standable and even expected. She would leave well-enough alone.

By the time Lydia arrived, and then Ralph, Maris and Cookie were seated with their breakfasts. Although good mornings were exchanged, Joseph kept his attention on his plate and remained quiet.

"This French toast is to die for," Lydia crowed as she went back for her second help-ing. "Cookie, you are wasted here."

"Oh, I don't know about that," Maris said quickly, smiling. "I think the mountain must come to Mohamed as far as the breakfast buffet of the B&B is concerned."

Cookie nodded at Lydia. "Thank you," she said, and looked at Maris. "And thank you." As she chopped into her cheese omelette with the side of her fork, she smiled. "I think I'll stay."

"Hey, Lydia," Ralph said. "I don't suppose you've snorkeled the bay, have you?"

"No," she said, taking her seat again. "Why, are you thinking of it?"

"I am," he replied, getting up with his plate, "but I'm not familiar with the currents, and where might be the best spot."

"For snorkeling?" Joseph said. "You're good on the currents anywhere near the south end. But for clarity, I'd dive closer to the center."

"Oh," Ralph said, sounding pleasantly surprised. "Are you a diver, Joseph?"

The lawyer cast a quick glance at Maris before answering. "Let's just say I picked it up after having done a little diving related to my work. I also happen to be privy to certain assessments regarding this bay's currents.

Frankly, it'd make for a great snorkeling spot."

As the three of them chatted about snorkeling and other kinds of diving, Maris noted that they were all careful to avoid recent events. While Lydia and Ralph talked about their jobs, she assumed that they already knew what the corporate lawyer did and who he worked for. As Maris was finishing her juice, Toler's phone rang. He frowned at the Caller ID before answering.

"Toler," he said. Then he glanced at Maris. "Good morning, Sheriff."

He quickly got up and went into the library, but his voice carried. "Spear fishing?" There was silence for a few moments. "Well, yes. I would think that'd be the first person to question." Again there was silence. "Yes, at the tackle shop." Maris knew they had to be talking about Ryan Quigg. "All right. Thanks for keeping me in the loop."

Maris exchanged a look with Cookie. It sounded as though the murder weapon might have been a spear from a fishing gun, and that Ryan was a suspect.

But what neither Mac nor Joseph knew was that Ryan wouldn't be at his shop until later. At this very moment, he'd be where he was every morning—fishing at the pier.

She gathered up her glass, tea cup, and plate. "I'm going to go run an early errand," she said to Cookie. To Lydia and Ralph she said, "I hope you enjoy your day."

9

———

After the foggy drive around the bay, Maris parked in the pier's lot—where she'd been chatting with Mac only yesterday. Despite Audrey's death, several cars were parked, and it seemed that it was mostly business as usual. Maris pulled the collar of her jacket up against the misty chill and headed to the pier. As she strolled past the various fishermen with lines dropped over the rail, she took a quick look in their buckets.

"Good looking perch," she said to a woman in a bright purple hoodie. The striped yellow of the fish was unmistakable.

"Thanks," she replied, smiling. "They're really biting today."

Maris moved on to the next fisherman, an

older man in an olive drab coat and matching ball cap. "Morning," he said to her with a little nod.

"Ooh," she said, looking down at a couple dozen small, sleek, silvery fish. "The jacksmelt seem to be swarming this morning."

"They're biting pretty well," the man agreed, as Maris moved on.

Checking the morning's fresh catch was something that Maris had done with Aunt Glenda. One morning a week, they'd pick up coffee and a pastry and then walk the foggy pier. It was Glenda who'd taught her how to recognize all the fish.

"Flounder," Maris said, looking into the next container. "Great for stuffing."

The flat bottom dweller had a mottled brown coloring that perfectly mimicked the sand. A young couple that she didn't recognize occupied the railing in front of the bucket, both bundled up and huddled together. They had also caught a few perch.

"Good for poaching too," the young woman said, smiling.

"Mmm," Maris said, as she passed them by. "That sounds good."

Finally though, she came to Ryan, with his two ten-gallon buckets.

Not only had he caught flounder, perch, and jacksmelt, but also sand dabs. They looked a lot like flounder but without the blotchy look. She gave a low whistle.

"Nice catch," she said.

As his rod bent downward and he cranked the reel, he grinned at her. "Always."

As far as Maris could tell, that was true. Ryan had an uncanny ability with the rod and reel. Sometimes it looked as though he could simply lower an empty hook in the water and catch the fish of his choice. If Maris's guess didn't miss its mark, the young redhead was one of the magic folk. Unfortunately, Pixie Point Bay etiquette considered direct questions about a person's magic ability rude.

She smiled at him. "You must eat well at lunch."

But the thin young man shook his head, even as he reeled in another jacksmelt. "I donate most of mine to the other fishers." He nodded down the line of buckets she'd just walked past, all heads turned to watch Ryan haul in another fish.

"That's very nice of you," she said.

"I'm one of those people that doesn't fish for the fish," he said, grabbing the jacksmelt and unhooking it from the artificial lure. "If you know what I mean."

She leaned back against the railing and crossed her arms. "Then why is it that you fish?"

He smirked at her. "It's what I have instead of meditation." He cranked the lure and weight up a bit tighter, leaned back with the rod, and whipped it overhead. Maris turned to watch as the nylon line sailed through the air in a beautiful arc. It landed some twenty yards in the distance with a little plop. He cranked the reel a few times, then set the pole down. "Listen."

Maris did. Water gently lapped against the pier's moorings below. Somewhere in the fog a seagull cried. As Maris looked to the south, she saw the steadily revolving beam of her lighthouse in the distance. The sun was just a dim glow, low on the horizon in the east. She heard the crank of fishing reels, and a small exclamation of triumph.

She gazed back at Ryan to see his sea

green eyes watching her. "A beautiful meditation," she agreed, "if ever I've heard one."

"Pixie Point Bay is more than a great place to fish, or a tourist destination." The young man shrugged. "I don't really know how to put it into words, but it's more than the sum of its parts. Way more." His pole dipped suddenly, and he snatched it up.

As Maris watched him catch yet another fish, she recalled how angry he and Howard had been yesterday. She was just beginning to glimpse how much a part of Ryan's life the bay was. He unhooked a sand dab this time.

"It's hard to imagine your meditation with an oil derrick in it," she said.

He froze, and jerked his gaze up to her face. "Hard to imagine? I can imagine it only too well." His jaw went tight. "Imagine the sound of the drill right now. Imagine the engines of a tanker. Even in the fog, we'd just be able to make out the rig too. Let's not even mention all the helicopters that will come and go, and all the damage to the seabed where these fellows live." He raised the sand dab and then gently slipped it into the bucket. "It would be the end of Pixie Point Bay."

"Audrey Graisser was killed with a spear from a spear fishing gun," she said abruptly.

Ryan had been cranking up the lure and weight, but paused. He cast a long sideways glance at her. "Is that right?"

Although Maris didn't think for one instant that the young fisherman would be capable of murder, it wasn't exactly the kind of shocked reaction she'd expected.

Clearly he wasn't shocked.

"You wouldn't happen to know anything about spear fishing guns, would you, Ryan?"

"I prefer a rod and reel, myself," he said, not looking at her. He swung the rod behind him and cast the line. "I also prefer dry land."

"She was killed on dry land," Maris said.

Again Ryan paused and averted his gaze. "You don't say."

"Actually, not me," she said. "The sheriff." She waited for that to sink in. "In fact, he'll be paying you a visit when your shop opens. So you might want to figure out what you're going to say about spear fishing guns."

His mouth pressed into a thin line before he finally turned to her. "One was stolen from my shop."

Maris arched her brows at him. "A spear fishing gun? When?"

He shook his head, and looked away, his jaw tight. "I don't know. Recently."

That was a lie. It'd been stolen, all right, and he probably knew exactly when.

He'd fixed his gaze firmly on where the line had landed and continued to hold the pole instead of setting it down. Maris had the distinct impression that their little chat was over.

"Just FYI," she said, turning to go, "he'll take your fingerprints, but it's just routine."

He looked at her, and nodded a little. "Thanks for the heads-up." Then his face clouded a little. "I guess I better make sure my fishing license is ready too."

10

Back at the B&B, Maris shifted into high gear with the usual to-do list. As she was heading upstairs, Cookie was heading downstairs with a load of dirty towels.

"Looks like everyone is out," Maris said, passing her with an empty trash bag in her hand.

"I didn't see Julia leave," the chef said, nodding, "but Joseph left shortly after Ralph and Lydia."

Upstairs in each of the rooms, Maris made and turned down the beds, tidied a little, and took out the trash. Cookie had already brought fresh towels and toiletries to the bathrooms.

In Julia's bedroom, as she emptied the

trash, something on the small rug in front of the dresser caught her eye. Though she bent to fetch it, she hesitated because she couldn't quite make out what it was. Instead, she took a tissue from the dispenser on the night stand, and used that to pick it up.

Though it was hard and looked somewhat like a shrunken acorn, it was mostly white. As she held it to the window light for a better look, she realized it was rock hard and hollow in the back. It wasn't an acorn, of course, but she didn't know what it was—although it looked familiar.

As she slowly ambled back into the hallway, still holding it in the tissue, she paused.

"Oh, I wonder," she muttered, peering at it. "Hmm." Unfortunately she'd never paid particularly close attention to sea life. Someone else would have to identify it, so she carefully wrapped it up.

She took the gathered trash downstairs but left it in the hallway before heading back to her room to find her cell phone. From the frequently dialed numbers, she selected Mac's.

"Maris," he said. "Always good to hear from you."

She smiled. "Good to talk to you too." She looked down at the tissue. "I've come across something interesting here at the B&B, and I was wondering if you might want to stop by and have a look."

"Something?" he asked. "That sounds mysterious. What have you got?"

"Honestly, I'm not exactly sure."

There was a pause on the other end of the line. "Okay," he said. "How about this evening? My day is booked pretty solid."

"That'd be perfect," she said.

"Great," he replied. "See you then."

11

As Maris went back to the trash bag and started to take it outside, she passed the parlor, looked in, and stopped. Mojo was just hopping up to the coffee table that held the Ouija board. She held still. If ever she and Pixie Point Bay could use some help from the voices of the spirits, it was now.

Though she thought she'd been quiet, he surprised her by looking directly at her. His big orange eyes glittered and then he gave a rather loud version of his signature meow.

"Right," Maris said, depositing the trash bag in the hallway before she went into the parlor. "Here I am."

She gave his head a single, gentle rub be-tween the ears, and he quickly sat next to the board. But rather than lift his paw to the planchette, he licked it and then rubbed it over his face. Hands on hips, she glared at him.

"Tell me I wasn't summoned, front and center, to watch you bathe." But as he continued his ablutions, it seemed that was exactly what had happened. "Honestly, Mojo," she said. "I really don't–"

As though he sensed she'd be leaving in the next instant, he put his paw down and went still.

Though she'd been ready to turn and leave, she paused. Slowly his gaze lifted to the opposite wall, and fixed itself there. His whiskers, which she'd never noticed during one of these sessions, drooped a little.

Was he relaxing?

His unblinking eyes were focused on something in the distance, something that Maris suspected was far beyond the wallpaper or even the confines of the house. Meanwhile though, his ears easily made up for the thousand-yard stare. They went into overdrive, the soft triangles swiveling to and fro, hearing something or listening for something, Maris didn't know which. As she watched, it even seemed as though he sighed.

She cocked her head at him. Either she hadn't been paying close enough attention in the past or he'd changed his routine.

Then, ever so slowly, his front paw reached out and came down lightly on the heart shaped planchette. He moved it, in a stately pace, from the middle of the board closer to him, stopping over the X.

"What in the world?" Maris whispered.

X-ray...or maybe Xerox, she thought, only to have her guesses thwarted by the next letter, on the opposite side of the board: A.

She scowled and shook her head. 'XA' made no sense whatsoever. Even stranger was the way he was going from one side of the board to the other, because the planchette slid all the way back to him, landing on the 'V.'

Maris almost laughed. This could not be a clue.

As the planchette began another journey back across the board, it abruptly stopped in the middle: I.

She frowned down at the letter under the plastic lens, wracking her brain. Though she'd never been great at spelling or word games, this was simply insoluble.

But the next two letters were close to the 'I.' In quick succession the planchette paused over the 'E' and then 'R' before Mojo took his paw from it.

"Xavier," she whispered.

It wasn't a word, as such, but rather a name.

Mojo blinked up at her, then stood. He took a moment to shake out his fur, and jumped down to the floor. Though she knew it would do no good, she was compelled to ask anyway.

"Xavier Who?" she said to him, following him out to the hall.

He didn't even look back, but headed to their bedroom and disappeared into it.

She cupped a hand around her mouth. "Thanks just the same."

As she turned back to the trash and picked it up, she had no idea who Xavier might be. But the one thing she did know was that, whoever he was, he'd be important.

At that moment, Cookie emerged from the pantry, with a piece of paper in her hand.

On it, Maris could see that the chef's elegant handwriting had created a list.

"Are you going into town any time soon?" the older woman asked. "If not, this can wait. It's just the usual."

Maris thought for a moment. "I'd be delighted to make the shopping run," she said. "Let me just take out the trash, and I'll get that list from you."

Who knows, she thought. Maybe she'd run into Xavier.

12

By the time Maris had gone up and down every aisle of the market, her cart was getting full. It was often the case that there'd be a long shopping list when the B&B was running close to capacity, but right now, it definitely wasn't. Instead, Maris knew what was happening. From her initial loss of appetite on the day Audrey had been killed, she'd already switched to anxiety eating. Sparked by the special Belgian chocolate the previous night—and how wonderfully comforting it'd been—she'd added her favorite candy bar to the basket, along with some chunks of dark chocolate, and fudge cookies. As usual, her chocolate superpower had led her to all the best. She wheeled her cart to the checkout.

"Did you find everything you need?" Howard asked.

If Maris wasn't mistaken, his billowing white hair looked a bit more flyaway than usual.

"And then some," Maris said, taking out the fresh vegetables first.

Rather than ring them up, however, Howard went to the long wood counter where the big glass jars of hard candy were set up in a long row. Although there seemed to be every color of the rainbow and every flavor, he went directly to the big jar with the beige and brown spiral sticks. Using a piece of wax paper, he took one out.

When he brought it back to her, he was beaming. "A barber pole for the little lady."

Maris grinned back. He never forgot. It'd been their ritual since she'd been just a girl.

"Well," she said, accepting the root beer candy. "Not so little any more, but always grateful." She popped the end in her mouth. "Thank you," she said around it.

The diet was definitely going to have to wait.

As Howard rang up her goods, she noticed the flyers next to the cash register. But even from a distance she could tell they were not the same flyers they'd used during the rally. She moved closer. Although at the top the bold letters said, 'STOP THE RIG' as had the others, below there was some type of technical illustration. Clearly it was the silhouette of a giant boat with the bay below it, and it seemed to be dragging some type of long pod or maybe a small submarine behind it. Giant circles emanated from it.

Maris frowned a little. Was it sonar?

Some items in the illustration were labeled, but what really drew her eye was the massive lettering at the bottom: 'NAP KILLS.' The entire illustration between the two lines of text was circled with a slash going through it.

"What do you think?" Howard asked her as he bagged the groceries.

She tilted her head. "Well, I think the message is pretty clear."

"Exactly," he said nodding. "I'd like nothing better than to clobber them with science, but people won't read a journal publication."

"Is this something you've researched?" she asked.

"Of course," he exclaimed. "Everyone should." He paused for a second and looked around the shop, which made Maris do the same. They were alone. "Don't get me wrong. I'm sorry that poor girl died. But her death shows you exactly how important it is to keep NAP out of the bay. It's deadly important. The bay would die."

"Die?" Maris said, taking out her barber pole. "As in, die?"

"The EIRs are useless," he declared, his voice rising. "What about the disruption to wildlife? And I'm not talking about the species in the water. We've also got to worry about air pollution, noise pollution, and light pollution. Do you think the people here in the vicinity are going to be breathing clean air?" Before Maris could answer, he plunged on. "No. So we'll either suffer with it and risk our health or leave." He flung his arm toward the front of the store. "But the oaks and red-woods? They can't leave."

As his voice took on an angry edge, Maris noticed the protest signs. He'd kept a couple and they were taped to the shelves behind the counter.

"And don't you believe for a minute that

the only thing to fear is an oil spill," he said, jamming his finger down on the digital tablet that served as his new checkout system. "Just the construction of an oil derrick is going to wreak havoc. Period. The bay will die."

Maris took out her credit card and handed it to him. He swiped it through the reader with such force, she thought it might burst into flames.

"It may not be a popular opinion to voice any more," he said, handing back her card. "But I'm as violently opposed to NAP as ever." She signed the tablet. "Maybe more so." He printed her receipt, and ripped it off. "Frankly, that guest of yours is a hero." Maris arched her eyebrows at him. "Julia Mendes, I mean. She's the one we ought to be talking about. In my opinion, she's done a stupendous job."

As he handed her the receipt, Maris managed a smile. "I'll, um, let her know." Despite how angry he was at the rally, Howard's tirade had taken her by surprise. She raised the candy to him. "Thanks again."

As she turned to go, he said, "Any time and you let her know!"

13

As Maris put away the perishables in the fridge and then the pantry and cleaning supplies, she separated out the chocolate, keeping it in a small bag. She'd done well over the last number of months—with an early backslide or two—but she'd always been a stress eater. Everything about Audrey Graisser's death had been stressful, starting with the possibility that an oil derrick might drill in the bay, then the young woman's tragic death, and now the townsfolk being painted with a broad brush as somehow being responsible. Add to that the fact that Claribel had warned her, and yet she'd been unable to prevent it.

In her room, Mojo was taking his usual afternoon nap on the bed, but picked up his head at the sound of the rustling of the bag. Though she didn't want to wake him, she was starving. She took out a candy bar, opened it, and took a bite—and had to roll her eyes.

"So good," she muttered. The caramel was perfectly soft, the nuts perfectly crunchy, the nougat perfectly smooth, and the chocolate—well, perfectly chocolaty. As she sat down at the desk, she noticed Mojo watching her with what seemed like a look of disapproval. "What?" she demanded.

The food guilt was bad enough without any added feline recrimination.

He gave her a short little meow, jumped down from the bed, trotted over, and jumped up to her lap. There he circled once and settled right down. His satisfied purr rumbled quietly and she had to smile. There'd been no recrimination, just an opportunity for a better napping spot.

Maris softly stroked his back. "Thanks, Mojo."

But as she enjoyed the rest of the bar, she recalled the market, particularly the flyer that Howard had put together. She tapped her temple and used her photographic memory to bring up an image of it. She stroked Mojo's back as she took a minute to actually read the labels on the illustration. It did sound a bit like a science paper, which wasn't too surprising. Nor was the fact that she wasn't familiar with some of the terms.

She frowned a little. "Air guns and sonic waves."

Her gaze landed on her laptop and she decided to educate herself. As Howard had said, they all ought to be doing some research.

She opened the computer and booted it up, then went to a search engine and typed in "air guns sonic waves." The first link looked promising and she clicked on it. As she read about seismic surveys, her curiosity turned to dismay. The method of using an air gun to produce enormous pulses of sound killed plankton as far away as one kilometer.

"Good grief," she said, leaning forward.

Mojo gave a forlorn little meow before jumping down.

She put down the bar and started scrolling. More than fifty percent of the tiny creatures were killed outright—not to mention the knock-on effect of animals higher in the food chain also dying. But the real clincher was the sonic effect on the gentle creatures who used sound for communication and were finely tuned to detect it. It was nothing short of a bomb blast. Whales had actually been known to avoid those areas, going so far as to halt migrations 175 kilometers away.

As one click led to another, she found herself on web pages with original journal articles and wondered if perhaps Howard had authored one. But as she kept an eye out for his name, it came up in a completely different context: he had a related patent.

"Hmm," Maris muttered, doing a quick search for the patent. When she found it, she had to blink. "A new oil drilling technology?"

Though she didn't understand the details, it looked like satellites could be used to spot oil leaks from abandoned underwater wells. But the same technology had been used to detect wells whose construction had never been finished, but were already approved, and could be started up again rapidly. In fact, the oil company that had used this patented satellite technology to resurrect old wells was synonymous with environmental disaster, having perpetrated the largest oil spill in history. Even today, birds on that part of the Gulf of Mexico were being rescued from an oil-sodden death, while the sludgy bodies of sea turtles and dolphins regularly washed ashore.

Maris sat back in her chair. No wonder Howard was so opposed to the oil well. He'd inadvertently been involved with one of the most lethal spills in history.

But did that translate to violence?

Maris shook her head. "No," she whispered.

She'd known Howard too long. He was simply not capable. She glanced at the computer screen. But she was going to have to ask him about this. With a sigh, she finished off the last of the candy bar. Good thing she'd bought more.

14

When Maris got up from the desk, she found that Mojo had decided to perch in the bay window. Luckily, her little cat preferred to interact with nature remotely. In the beginning she'd been worried that he might be an escape artist and scooped him up every time he was in the vicinity of open doors. But it hadn't taken long, with the guests coming and going, until she'd simply been too far away to pick him up. But to her relief, he'd trotted to the threshold, looked out, and then trotted away before the door closed. At this point she wondered if he'd even put up with being carried outside—not that she wanted to encourage him.

"What do your kitty eyes see?" she asked him.

Following his line of sight, Maris looked south along the coast, and then at the lawn that bordered the B&B. A small squirrel seemed to be foraging in the grass. It tucked its nose to the ground, in between the green blades, but periodically checked the surroundings. Slowly it was crossing from right to left, and Mojo was watching.

But as Maris watched him watch, she realized it wasn't a predatory or hunting type of interest. His whiskers didn't twitch; he seemed relaxed; and he certainly didn't hunker low. It was almost as though he was watching television. Then again, the pudgy black cat had no need of hunting, since she and Cookie kept him constantly supplied with the only thing he would eat: smoked salmon.

"At least you've got good taste," she said, as she stroked his head.

When she turned away from the window, she saw the black skeleton key that hung next to the door. It'd been weeks since she'd been in the basement. After having spent a bit of time in the cellars of Alegra Winery, she'd felt she'd been making good progress on confronting her mild claustrophobia. But her trip into the dark space below floor level had still created the anxiety that it always had, just not as much. The real reason she'd first gone down there, though, was to search for her aunt's beautiful green pendulum. Conspicuous by its absence from the silk brocade box on top of the armoire, Maris still thought of it from time to time —like now.

She strode to the door and took the key before she could think of an excuse not to go investigating. As she went to the utility room, Mojo jumped down from his perch and followed her. If she had to guess, she'd say he enjoyed these little jaunts. He sat down next to the big metal lock, his nose almost on it.

"Careful of those whiskers," she said, and inserted the key and turned it.

The familiar grinding of the heavy mechanism greeted them, and Mojo cocked his head in response. She frowned a little at him. He'd heard this dozens of times before. Why be puzzled by it now? Was it different? As she continued turning the lock, she listened intently. Although he kept tilting his head, one way and then the other, it sounded no different to her.

It was unnerving.

Finally, when the key turned freely, the clunking and scraping stopped, and Mojo simply looked up at her.

"Honestly, Mojo. Sometimes you worry me."

He scratched lightly at the lock.

"Okay, okay," she said. "Here we go."

Grasping the thick black handle, she tugged open the wood hatch.

Mojo immediately bolted down the stairs.

"Uh, after you," she said, and leaned the door off to one side.

As she looked down at the steps descending into darkness, it occurred to her that the electricity might not be working down there either.

Good grief, she thought. That would be a deal breaker.

Her mild claustrophobia was the result of being trapped in an elevator without power, in the dark and in silence. There was no way in the world she'd repeat that.

She crept down the few steps that it took to reach the light switch and flicked it on. To her relief, the long fluorescent bulbs beneath her popped to life. But as she looked down at the well lit area, she also found she was a little disappointed. Her excuse to abandon this foray was gone.

"You don't have to stay long," she told herself, as the familiar tightening in her chest began. "Just a minute or two. Mojo's not afraid."

Then again, she thought, *he'd probably never been trapped in an elevator.*

She passed the collection of beautiful antique books in the diagonal bookcase to her left, not pausing to look at them. Instead, she proceeded directly to the floor and took a step away from the stairs.

So far, so good. She hadn't even broken out in a sweat.

The familiar hat boxes, crates, dresser, and suitcase looked exactly as they always had. But as she looked past them, she saw Mojo sitting on top of one of the steamer trunks. He gave her a plaintive little mew, his big orange eyes seeming to catch all the light from the bulbs overhead.

"That one?" she asked him. It was further

into the basement than she'd ever gone. "Are you sure?"

For an answer, he simply stared at her.

She glanced back over her shoulder and up to the utility room, and then back at the little cat, who hadn't moved.

"Okay, fine," she muttered, and hurried to the antique trunk.

Laying on its side, it was still as tall as her waist. It was the kind of luggage rarely seen anymore, though she'd seen one or two still in use in her hospitality days. As the name implied, it was the type of trunk used on steamer ocean crossings, and had to hold a lot. The latch was unlocked, and as she lifted it, Mojo jumped up to the nearby suitcase.

Though Maris fully expected it to be chock full of his toys, she was pleasantly surprised at what she found.

"Photos," she whispered.

Some were in plastic sleeves—like the one of her from her senior year in high school—while others were in all sorts of frames. Under those were several photo albums, as well as some manilla envelopes and archival boxes. Judging from the size of the trunk, there might be several hundred photographs here.

Idly, she moved aside her senior portrait and one of the envelopes, and found herself looking at Aunt Glenda. It was always like looking in a mirror. They had the same blue eyes and strawberry blonde hair; the same heart-shaped face and petite nose; and the same decidedly non-petite figure. The shag haircut that Glenda wore, along with the Gunne Sax blouse and faded colors of the photo, indicated it might have been taken in the seventies. The heavily tarnished silver frame said the same. But the real icing on this photographic cake was Cookie.

The two friends were posing in the parlor, in front of the record player. Cookie's hair was shoulder length and jet black, and she wore a floral apron over a crew-neck t-shirt and a pair of faded bell-bottom jeans. Glenda had her arm over the chef's shoulders, and Cookie had wrapped an arm around her friend's waist. Their smiles positively glowed, and Maris found herself smiling back at them. While the fashions and hair color had certainly changed, the parlor hadn't, right down to the furniture and records.

Maris realized that Mojo hadn't moved from his nearby perch and looked up at him. "Nothing you want to explore?" she said, and turned to look at the rest of the basement— which is when the sweat started.

As the familiar tightening in her chest also began, Maris clutched the framed photo to her chest.

"On second thought..." Slowly, she lowered the trunk's big lid and looked up at her cat. "Good find," she told him. "Let's go."

He apparently needed no more urging. As fast as he'd come down, he shot up the stairs, and Maris followed close behind.

BACK IN HER ROOM, Maris adjusted the photo of Glenda and Cookie on her dressing table. She knew exactly where the silver polish was kept. It wouldn't take long to get the pretty frame lustrous once more. But as she rubbed a thumb over a particularly dark spot, the entire room disappeared in a hazy cloud of white.

She froze.

Rather than knock the picture over, she

slowly removed her hand from it. By now she'd learned that the onset of her magical ability—the precognition that she'd also shared with Glenda—meant she no longer saw her surroundings.

Early in life, she'd assumed that everyone occasionally had 'flashes of insight.' But since returning to Pixie Point Bay, she'd learned and accepted that she was a witch, as were her family members before her. Now her moments of precognition were not only welcome, but wanted. She relaxed her shoulders and back as the vision coalesced in front of her.

"By Hook or Crook," she murmured.

It was the crochet club located on the Towne Plaza. The charming three story Victorian—white with gray and red roof tiles, along with smart black trim—was also the home of the club's president, Millicent Leclair. In her early eighties, Millicent was not just the head of the club, or simply an aura reader, she was the leader of a cabal of crafty and cunning eavesdroppers and observant onlookers. If anyone had ears and eyes on what happened in Pixie Point Bay, it was these older ladies.

In the next moment the vision evaporated, and Maris was looking once again at the portrait. She smiled at it, and then at herself in the dressing table mirror. It seemed the polish would have to wait. Instead, she'd need to dig out her crochet project.

But then the front doorbell rang.

15

"Come in, Mac," Maris said, smiling as she opened the door. "Thank you for stopping by."

"My pleasure," he said, smoothing down his tie. "As always."

As she closed the door, he waited for her. "Let me go get it," she said. She indicated the library. "Please, make yourself comfortable and I'll be right back."

"Thanks," he said, as they went their separate ways.

In her bedroom, she carefully picked up the tissue wrapped item. When she arrived in the living room, Mac turned from the bookshelf as she entered. Gently, she placed the little bundle in his outstretched palm. He opened the tissue by unfurling each corner until the center was revealed.

He peered more closely. "I think that's a barnacle," he said, turning it over without touching it.

She nodded. "I'm no expert on marine life but, if I'm not mistaken, that's the kind that grows under the pier."

"Or on the boats moored there," he suggested. "Or the rocks nearby."

Maris pursed her lips, considering. She hadn't thought of those other sources.

The sheriff removed a small evidence bag from a front trouser pocket. With just one hand, he opened the top and slipped both the tissue and crusty barnacle inside. Then he sealed the top.

"Where did you find it?"

"In Julia's room," she replied. "I was tidying and taking out the trash, like usual. I found it on the rug."

"Good eye," he said, lifting the bag to the window light. "It'd be hard to spot."

"It had a strange look to it, even from across the room."

"I'm guessing," he said, lowering it, "that

since there are no other cars out front, that Julia isn't here."

Maris nodded. "Right. It's hard to say when she'll be back."

"No problem," Mac said, regarding her. "I've had a chance to talk with Ryan and Howard." He raised a single eyebrow. "It seems as though I'm always the second person to interview suspects. Some unnamed personage always manages to get there before me."

Maris felt warmth rising to her cheeks. "Well, it's just that...that..."

Mac held up a hand, smiling. "It also hasn't escaped my notice that Pixie Point Bay is a pretty tight-knit community—one that you're part of." He grinned a little more broadly. "'May secrecy round be the mystical bound, and brotherly love be the center.'"

She grinned back at him. "Burns?"

He nodded. "You got it. Old Rabbie knew a thing or two about secrecy." He gazed at her. "You've got a good head for investigating, which is not that common."

Now she felt like her face must be glowing. What Mac called 'having a good head' was really mostly magic. Not only did she have her precognition, but between Mojo's clues and Claribel's insights, she could hardly go wrong. But she couldn't argue the fact that, no matter how she got it done, she did in fact manage to solve crimes.

"Thanks," was all she managed to say.

Mac smoothed his tie again, and adjusted the clip, though it wasn't needed. For a moment or two there was an awkward silence as he stared at his shoes.

"I was wondering," he finally said, raising his gaze to her face. "If maybe you'd be available for lunch tomorrow?"

A thrilling little zing shot up her spine. "I'd be delighted," she answered, almost before he'd finished the question.

He smiled at her. "Great."

Maris didn't even know what day tomorrow was, but if she'd had something scheduled, she'd change it. "Great," she echoed.

"I'll pick you up at noon?" he asked, turning to the door.

"Perfect," she said, as they went into the hall. "Noon it is."

He nodded. "I'll let myself out, and see you tomorrow, then."

"I'll look forward to it," she said.

As Maris stood in the hallway watching Mac head to the front door, it opened ahead of him. Julia Mendes stepped through, saw the two of them, and stopped. For a moment she stared at them, then turned to close the door. Maris had the sudden impression she'd bolt through it if she thought she could get away.

But when she headed to the stairs, Mac spoke. "Ms. Mendes. Just the person I wanted to see."

Again she came to a halt and stared at them. "Oh?" She glanced between them. "And why is that? Have you found the murderer?"

Mac shook his head and produced the evidence bag. "I'd like to show you something."

He held it out in front of her and she peered at it, then frowned. "What is it?" She looked around the bag at him, waiting.

"It's a barnacle," he replied, watching her.

She cocked her head a little and frowned. "Oh, a barnacle. Okay. You have a barnacle."

He lowered it. "It was found in your room."

Her eyebrows flew up. "In my room?" She glanced at the ceiling. "You mean upstairs?" The sheriff nodded, not saying anything. Julia scowled. "You searched my room? Doesn't that require–"

"I found it," Maris interrupted. "I was turning down the bed and taking out the trash. It was on the floor and I picked it up to throw it away."

"Oh," Julia said, somewhat subdued. "Okay, fine. There was a barnacle on my floor."

"The kind that one might find under a pier, for example," Mac said.

Julia crossed her arms and glowered at him. "A pier where someone was murdered, for example."

"Possibly," he replied calmly.

"I see," she said, her jaw clenching. "And I suppose someone would have waded into the water, scraped it off some wood, and then taken it as a souvenir."

"Or it would have stuck to the bottom of someone's shoe," Mac replied.

Julia jabbed a finger at it. "That? On the bottom of a shoe without knowing it?" She glared at Maris as well. "Are you joking?" She crossed her arms again. "Because it's really not that funny."

"In fact," Mac said, "I'm deadly serious. Can you tell me why this was in your room?"

She shook her head and smirked. "Because it was stuck to the bottom of someone else's shoe." She eyed Maris, but then returned her gaze to the sheriff. "Other than that, I have no idea."

Mac nodded. "All right, Ms. Mendes. I don't have any other questions for you now."

The young woman seemed as though she was going to make some retort, but then thought better of it. Without a word, she brushed past them and then up the stairs. Then her door slammed.

Maris grimaced a little. "She has a point. I'm pretty sure I'd feel that under my shoe."

"*Under* the shoe," Mac said, "I'd agree. But what if it'd been caught on some laces, or stuck to the side." He lifted the evidence bag again. "First, though, I'll see if it can be identified. We'll go from there."

Maris nodded. "Sounds good."

He smiled at her. "This time I really will see myself out."

She laughed a little. "Okay, see you tomorrow."

16

———

To the west, the sun had begun its slow descent to the sea, which meant that it was time to start assembling the cheeseboard, and thinking about some wine pairings. Maris went to the kitchen and opened the large brushed steel door. Although Julia might not be joining them this evening, no doubt Ralph and Lydia would be partaking, and perhaps Joseph. Then again, Maris hoped that Julia would surprise her and indeed come down, since she would very likely have something in common with Ralph and his globe-trotting adventure blog.

She let her gaze wander over the various cheeses but then found herself looking at Mojo's smoked salmon. It might be nice to have a little company as she got ready for the Wine Down. She picked up the plastic container and gave it a little shake.

"Mojo," she called out. "Would you like a snack?"

This would be the second night in a row—and she didn't want to make this a habit—but it looked like she was also a stress feeder. She smiled when she heard his little paws padding down the hall.

"That's my boy," she said lowly, as she opened the container on the counter. "Are you ready for some salmon?"

Though she knew he'd come into the kitchen, and even heard him pad over to his bowl, he didn't answer. The one thing that Mojo always seemed ready to talk about was food, and yet he was silent. Maris frowned a little and turned to check on him.

There he sat, as usual, at his bowl, but in his mouth he had a tarot card. As he stared up at her with his big amber eyes, he dropped it in the empty bowl. Then he gave her his signature meow—and a loud one.

"Good grief," she said. "What have you got there?"

He gave her another meow, and placed

his paw on the card.

"Yeah," she said, "I can see it." She bent to pick it up, but then remembered the salmon. As she used a big spoon to take a portion, she said, "Tell you what. I'll trade you."

As she moved the spoon toward the bowl, Mojo lifted his paw from the card and she picked it up. Almost before the salmon landed in the bowl, Mojo dug in. She barely got the spoon back in time.

"Um, I'd say that's a fair trade."

As she set the spoon in the sink, she gazed down at the card—the six of pentacles. A rich man dressed in a red robe was handing out coins to two beggars who knelt at his feet. In the other hand, he held a scale that was balanced.

"Hmm," she muttered, and gave her temple a tap.

According to the small pamphlet of tarot interpretations that came with the deck, the scale represented fairness and equality. The six of pentacles meant that the tarot reader was either giving or receiving something, depending on where they were in the cycle of life.

She showed him the card. "So, is the rich

man supposed to be North American Petroleum?" He ignored her, still gulping down
his food. She turned it around to look at it
again. "Or are the six stars supposed to mean
something astronomical? Maybe six people?"

How many pylons were in an oil rig?

For all she knew, it could even be that
someone involved with the case might own a
red robe. No doubt it would all make sense
later, but that might be too late to salvage the
town's reputation or save the bay. She set the
card on the counter and stared down at it.

"Giving or receiving," she muttered.

Who was giving or receiving anything?

Mojo had finished his snack in record
time and now sat back, using his paw to clean
his face.

"You know, Mojo, maybe we should con-
sider a different process when it comes to the
tarot." When he ignored her, she sighed and
put the salmon back in the fridge. "Maybe
you'd like to actually deal a spread next
time."

This time he decided to answer her. As
she closed the fridge, he gave her a quick
little meow, and then trotted out of the room.

She smiled after him. "You're welcome."

17

Though it had seemed to take the sun forever to rise to its midpoint, noon was almost here. Maris had changed her outfit three times but finally settled on the cream blouse with the ruffled open collar, a navy blue cardigan over that, and a matching loose floral skirt. She almost never wore pants, so that choice had been easy. Not only did the dark background of the skirt match the cardigan, it had a nice slimming effect.

She gave her hair a final brush. In all the investigating into Audrey's death, Maris had forgotten about the blown fuse. Only when she'd returned to her room after the evening wine and cheese had she remembered. A quick phone call to Bear had assured her that he'd take a look at it later today.

But for now, she'd have to rough it without electricity. Cookie had been kind enough to lend her a hair dryer and the use of her bathroom. Meanwhile Maris's phone was charging in the kitchen. She looked at herself in the dressing table mirror and adjusted the pearl necklace.

As she checked her watch, the doorbell rang. She smiled as she got up. He was right on time. She grabbed her purse and hurried to the front, smiling more when she saw him through the door's window. It was the first time she'd seen him in casual attire instead of the sheriff's uniform.

"Mac," she said, as she opened the door. "What a nice outfit."

He wore black jeans and a light gray turtleneck that perfectly matched his eyes.

"I'm glad you think so," he said, looking down at himself. "I don't have much opportunity to dress down, so to speak." He moved his gaze to her skirt, her blouse, and then her face. "You, however, are looking your same wonderful self. No need to change a thing." He thought for a moment. "'Her look was like the morning's eye, her air like nature's vernal smile.'"

She had to grin at the compliment, via Burns, of course. "Let me just get my phone."

As he stepped inside, she went to the kitchen, unplugged the phone, and dropped it in her purse. Back at the entry, she slung it over her shoulder. "Ready when you are."

"Let's go," he said, holding the door for her.

Not only had she never seen him out of uniform, but she'd never seen his car—or rather truck. Though she knew little about makes and models of vehicles, it had the look of something more recent. It was big but sleek, and its simple black color seemed to match his attire. He opened the passenger door for her and indicated a dark metal rail that ran just below it.

"Use the running board," he said indicating it, and held out his hand to her. "There's also a handhold there." He pointed to a handle just above the window.

Maris gladly took his hand, and put her foot on the running board. It was deceptively high. She bounced a little to give herself just a bit of momentum, but it was too much. Before she could duck through the door, she bumped her head on the roof.

"Oh no," Mac said. As she plopped onto the passenger seat at an angle, he put a steadying hand on her arm. "Are you okay?"

She pushed down on the seat to right herself, only to find she was pushing on her skirt. "I'm fine," she said, her voice straining as she tried to get up, even as she pinned the skirt to the seat.

"The handle," Mac said gently. He patted it, now next to her head.

"Oh, right," she said quickly reaching for it—and giving him an elbow in the face. "*Mac*," she exclaimed, as he backed up. Though he was smiling, he touched a finger under his nose. "Are you all right?"

He examined his finger, which had no blood, and laughed a little. "Perfectly fine."

Gripping the handle, she was finally able to sit up straight and get the skirt untangled underneath her. "Are you sure?" she said.

He nodded. "Just a bump." He stepped back. "Watch the door." Slowly, he closed it.

By the time he'd climbed into the driver's seat, Maris had managed to regain a bit of composure. Though her face felt like it was on fire, she tugged on her safety belt, careful to keep her grip on it.

"Just thank goodness Cookie is inside," she said, "or I'd have found a way to flail around and hit her too."

Mac chuckled. "Note to self: Next time, bring a couple of helmets."

Now Maris had to laugh too. For a few seconds, that's all they did. She liked the way his eyes crinkled when he laughed—and that he was already thinking of a next time.

"Okay," he finally said, putting on his belt and turning on the engine. "We've got a reservation, so we'd better get going."

"A reservation?" Maris asked.

He nodded. "At Plateau 7."

18

A t the beautiful restaurant by the bay, Maris managed to exit the truck without incident. She and Mac had arrived on time, and she'd even managed not to die of embarrassment from her clumsiness. Although in reality, Mac made that easy. He'd chatted a bit about the case: Julia Mendes' fingerprints were on the flyers from under the pier but the spear had been clean; the analysis of the barnacle hadn't yet been completed, and no other evidence had surfaced.

Maris related the events at the B&B: neither Joseph nor Julia had been at the Wine Down the previous evening or this morning's buffet. She had concluded that, after the discovery of the barnacle and Julia's reaction to it, that either they didn't want to see each other, or possibly Maris, or they had their own reasons for not socializing. Any or all of those reasons would be perfectly understandable.

As the *maître d'* led them to a table next to one of the large windows, Maris had her first good look at the view. It was spectacular. The restaurant was perched on the edge of giant rough boulders, the surf seemingly just outside the window. From its vantage point midway on the semi-circle of the bay, she could look south and see the lighthouse and also north to the pier.

"What a stunning view," she said, as Mac held her chair for her and she took a seat.

"It's amazing," he agreed and seated himself.

The *maître d'* handed her a menu and then gave one to Mac. "Your server will take your order when you are ready, but may I get you something to drink?"

"Sparkling water for me," Maris said. The *maître d'* inclined his head to her.

"I'll have coffee," Mac said, "and regular water."

"Very good, sir," the man said with a little bow, before he left.

For several moments, neither of them looked at their menus, but instead gazed out at the bay. The wind must have been up since the azure blue of the waves was capped with tiny peaks of white. Two small sailboats leaned over at acute angles, cutting through the chop and leaving small wakes behind them. Occasionally a large enough wave would crash against the rocks just below the window and send up a fan of spray. Maris could have watched the scene forever.

"Maris Seaver," said a familiar voice. "What a pleasure."

Etienne Fournier, in his chef's hat and white uniform, was approaching the table. He carried a long, slim white platter with what appeared to be different pieces of sushi in a line down the middle.

He smiled as he set it down between them. "Compliments of the house."

"Oh how lovely," she said. She regarded the French owner of the restaurant and a former Cordon Bleu instructor. "Etienne Fournier, I don't know if you've met our county sheriff, Daniel McKenna."

The chef turned to him. "I have not had the pleasure," he said, extending his hand. "Sheriff, welcome to Plateau 7."

"Chef Fournier," Mac said. "The pleasure is mine."

As the two men shook hands, Maris glanced at the long tray and realized it wasn't sushi at all. The chef must have seen her surprised expression. He smiled, which brought up the small points of his mustache.

"A petite sampler," he said, indicating the first *hors d'oeuvre*, which looked to Maris like a glistening, little, ruby red log. "Sweet lobster in a Madras curry oil." He moved on to the next. Like the first, it was also a cylinder but standing on end with a rounded top. "Roasted fingerling potato, filled with Greek yogurt and topped with caviar."

"Wow," Maris muttered.

"And finally," the chef declared, "the fish taco bite with creamy salsa drizzle." This last piece had the tiniest tostada shell Maris had ever seen, filled with a breaded cube of fish covered with white and red sauces. There were two of each of the small works of art.

"A masterful presentation," Maris said.

"Thank you, Chef," Mac added.

At that moment their server came to the table with the waters and Mac's coffee. Etienne stood aside.

"Would you like to order?" the young man said, smiling pleasantly.

"I'm afraid we haven't even opened the menus yet," Maris said.

"Of course," he said. "Please take your time."

When he'd departed, the chef said, "If I might make a suggestion?"

Though Mac had been opening his menu, he paused and looked at Etienne. "Yes, please."

"My signature dish is the salmon in sorrel sauce." His dark eyes glinted, and he pinched the air in front of him. "I use the thickest filets in the fish, baked with sorrel, finished with a shallot and white wine sauce. On the side is my award-winning *pomme puree* made from Yukon potatoes that are whipped until silky smooth." He looked at them both. "The fish was delivered two hours ago."

Mac closed his menu with finality. "How can I turn that down?"

The chef took his menu and Maris offered him hers as well. "That sounds perfect."

"*Bon*," he said, with a little nod, before departing for the kitchen.

Maris decided to sample the little potato with yogurt and caviar first. "Oh look," she said. "It's garnished with potato skins that have been fried." She popped the little delicacy in her mouth. The tang of the yogurt and the salt of the black caviar combined perfectly with the mild starch of the potato. "Mmm," she muttered.

Mac decided to try the lobster with Madras curry oil. "Just a little spicy," he said, "and a lot good." He looked out at the bay, a tranquil smile on his lips. "The best that small town life has to offer."

As Maris picked up the other lobster *hors d'oeuvre*, she said, "As I recall, you're from a little town up north called Pine Ridge."

He arched his eyebrows at her. "What a memory you have. Yes, that's right."

"But you'd worked in Los Angeles, before coming here."

He nodded, as he picked up the fish taco bite. "That was the last big city for me. I've sworn them off." He looked out at the panorama of the bay. "Too many people, too many cars, and not enough space. Crazy hours too. It was burnout, pure and simple. I saw this position come up, and jumped on it." He smiled at her. "Best decision I've made in my life." He popped the fish bite in his mouth, and Maris decided to try the lobster.

The chef and owner had really outdone himself. The flavors of each appetizer were incredibly different. She recalled how he'd explained the origin of his love of fresh seafood while teaching in Australia. He'd certainly found a way to express it here in Pixie Point Bay.

"As I recall," the sheriff said, "you were in Hong Kong the first time we spoke."

"That's right," Maris said. "I was at the premiere Far East holding of Luguan Imperial Resorts. That was my last big city as well." He looked at her quizzically. "I was their chief trouble-shooter. For a while, it was a resort a month." She grimaced at the memory. "Talk about burnout."

"You too?" he said, and sipped his coffee.

She nodded and recounted her many years in the hospitality industry, globe trotting and living out of a suitcase. The pay got better but the stress was insurmountable. The pace was grueling.

"It ultimately cost me a marriage," she finished.

Mac sat back in his chair as he nodded. "Me too," he said quietly.

She'd already known this about him, though he'd never told her.

"And now," she said, gesturing out to the water, "here we are in Pixie Point Bay."

He grinned. "Here we are," he echoed.

The chef reappeared, with their server in tow. "The sorrel salmon," he announced, taking a plate from the large silver tray that the young man held. He placed the dish in front of Maris. "Finished with a white wine and shallot sauce, and *pomme puree* on the side."

"It smells wonderful," she gushed, as the mild aroma of the fish wafted over her, accompanied by the tang of sorrel, almost like wild strawberries.

Etienne placed the other plate in front of Mac, as the server cleared the *hors d'oeuvres* plate.

"Those appetizers were as magnificent," Mac said to the chef, "as this view."

"Yes," Maris agreed. "What a wonderful selection. Thank you."

Though the chef smiled a little and bowed to accept the compliment, when he rose, his brow was furrowed. "Of course, both may vanish if we cannot stop this insanity of an oil well." He nodded to the bay. "Can you imagine this view with an oil derrick there?" He glanced at the table. "Or this meal without seafood?" He shook his head so fast that his chef's hat quivered. "Impossible."

"It won't happen," Maris told him. "We won't let it."

"I wish I could be so sure." He tossed his hands in the air. "And now with the death of that poor, unfortunate girl, we are the villains."

"The last word on that," Mac said, "hasn't been spoken. But the one thing I know is that we're going to get to the bottom of it."

The chef seemed to relax a little. "Of course," he said. "Of course. Please do not let me keep you from your food. *Bon appetit.*"

During the rest of lunch they enjoyed their food enormously and Maris recounted how she'd spent time in Pixie Point Bay with Aunt Glenda when she'd been younger. Mac asked about Mojo, and they laughed at some of his antics. But she couldn't shake the feeling that Etienne might be right. Suddenly, after all this time, Pixie Point Bay seemed like a fragile dream.

As though Mac had heard her thoughts, he said, "I know." She looked into his eyes and saw the same concern that she felt. "We can't let this end—and we won't."

She hadn't realized she'd stopped eating while she'd been staring out at the sparkling water, watching a pair of gulls swooping along the rocks. Now she saw that Mac hadn't finished his plate either.

With a little smile, she nodded. "Agreed."

He glanced at her dish. "Shall I get these to go?"

"That'd be great. Thank you, Mac."

As he signaled to the server for the check, she looked out at the bay again. He was right. It was unthinkable that this would end—so they simply would not let it.

19

Having managed to exit Mac's truck without causing bodily harm to anyone in the vicinity, Maris gave him a goodbye wave as he pulled away. It'd been a wonderful lunch, and he seemed to enjoy it just as much as her. As she went back into the B&B with her leftovers, she was already thinking that it'd be nice if she asked for a date next time—maybe pick him up at his place.

In the hallway, as she headed back to the kitchen, she heard a noise from the utility room. Bear's truck had been parked in front and she hoped that was him looking at the fuse. She stowed the salmon and potatoes in the fridge, went through her room, and into the utility room.

"Bear," she said. "It's good to see you."

Mojo was laying on top of his canvas tool bag, watching the big man. William "Bear" Orsino was what Maris would have pictured for a mountain man from a different era. With his full beard and outsized form, he was easily two heads taller than her. As usual he was dressed in a plain white t-shirt and blue bib overalls. Like many of the other people of Pixie Point Bay, Bear was one of the magic folk—a shifter—and he liked to be home before dark. But no matter what the B&B or lighthouse seemed to need, he was always up to the task.

"Hello, Maris," he said, turning to her but noticing Mojo.

"Let me get him out of there," Maris said, starting for him.

"Mojo is fine," he said, stopping her. "He looks so comfortable."

With his front paws tucked up under his chest and his eyelids half-closed, he looked like he'd made himself right at home.

Hands on hips, Maris gave her fluffy cat a disapproving look but left him where he was. She shifted her gaze to the fuse box. "Any progress?"

Bear nodded his big head. "Bad fuse." He tapped on it with the plastic handle of his screwdriver. "Right here."

She blinked at him. "You're kidding." Then she thought of the new appliance. "Had to have been my new hair dryer. It must have fried it." She was going to have to get a different one, maybe not so fancy and powerful. "So we'll need a new one?"

"Yes," he said. "I can pick it up at the hardware store in Cheeseman Village." He glanced at her, then at the ground, with a bit of a sheepish look on his face. "Tomorrow."

The trip there and back would make it late afternoon before he got around to replacing it, however long that would take. He'd want to be on his way home by then.

But there was no hurry. Living without electricity in her room wasn't so bad. She recalled a small hotel, early in her career, in the Scottish Highlands. After a record-breaking gale, the entire region had lost electricity for three days straight. Unfortunately, the water heater had needed electricity in order to function, and cold showers in the midst of winter had emptied the hotel in a hurry. At least here, she still had hot water.

"No problem," she said, smiling at Bear. "Whenever you can get to it is going to be fine."

Bear nodded with finality. "Tomorrow." He pocketed the screwdriver and went to his tool bag. With a gentleness that belied his powerful grip, he slipped his thick fingers underneath Mojo, and picked him up, his huge hands like a hammock for the little cat.

Maris held out her arms for the fluffy creature, which Bear slowly transferred to her. Mojo's eyes never even opened.

Quietly, Bear put the screwdriver away and closed the top of the bag. "Tomorrow," he whispered, before tiptoeing to the door.

Though Maris would never had guessed that work boots could be so quiet, he somehow managed to be almost silent. "See you tomorrow," she whispered back.

20

As Bear exited through the front door, Lydia and Ralph passed him coming in. Despite the fact that he was still tip-toeing, or maybe because of it, they gave him a wide berth and looked after him as he left.

When Lydia turned back, she saw Maris. "Oh good, we were hoping to catch you."

Both wore shorts and tank tops, carried backpacks, and looked tanned and relaxed. Suddenly, Maris thought of the fuse. "Why, did the electricity go off in your rooms?"

"No," Lydia said, and glanced at Ralph.

"Everything's fine in my room," he said.

"Oh," Maris said, relieved. At that moment, Mojo decided to wake up, stretch, and squirm to be put down—and Maris obliged him. "Then what is it that I can do for you?"

"Actually," Lydia said. "It's a perfect afternoon for paddleboarding. The wind's just died down. So we were wondering if you'd like to come along?"

"It really is fun," Ralph added. "You're going to like it."

Although Maris could think of a hundred things that needed to be done for the B&B, it wasn't the to-do list that gave her pause. It was the fact that she probably didn't own a bathing suit that fit any more. Even if she did, it was the last thing she'd want to be seen in.

Lydia saw her hesitation. "No gear necessary." She looked down at herself. "We're wearing what we've got on." She looked down at Ralph's hiking boots. "But I'm going to change into flip flops."

"Me too," Ralph said, nodding.

After the big lunch, it might be good to get some exercise. She knew she had shorts that fit. Hopefully they wouldn't be too unflattering. "All right," she said. "Should I meet you down at the pier behind the lighthouse?"

"Perfect," Lydia said, as she and Ralph headed to the stairs. "See you in a few."

"SAFETY FIRST," Lydia said. "This is your life vest."

Maris took what looked like a fanny pack from her. "This?" She held it up by one end. "A life vest?"

As Ralph strapped his on around his waist, the thick part in front, Lydia said, "It's a personal flotation device. You wear it like a belt, and pull the orange tab to inflate it."

Maris looped the belt around the outside of her tank top. As Lydia had suggested, she also wore flip flops, as well as a pair of—thankfully—baggy shorts. She clicked the buckle of the life vest together.

"If you land in the drink," Lydia explained, "and you pull the tab, an actual life vest pops out and is automatically inflated. You can put it on or cling to it." She patted her own belt. "These are great for kayaking and paddleboarding since they're not in the way."

Ralph crouched down at the edge of the pier, next to one of the paddleboards that were already in the water. They looked like really thick surfboards, though wider, and were grey with a fluorescent yellow trim.

As Maris watched, Ralph slowly moved sideways, almost on hands and knees, from the low dock onto the floating platform. Once aboard, he knelt and waited. He'd made it look so easy.

"Right," Lydia said. She gave him a wink. "I'm going to hire you as an assistant." She turned back to Maris. "Now we'll do the same." She pointed to a spot on the wood platform, next to another paddleboard. "Crouch down here. I'm going to hold the board."

"Okay," Maris said.

"There's no hurry," Lydia told her. "So take your time. These are all purpose paddleboards, extremely stable and quite unsinkable. It's like climbing onto a small boat."

Maris thought of the times she'd been aboard Slick's boat. She could expect it to move. But as she'd seen Ralph demonstrate, she crouched down, put one hand on the dock, and one on the board, along with one foot. With a wobble and moving a bit too fast, she moved sideways onto the board and knelt. Luckily, Lydia grabbed her arm to keep her from toppling over with the momentum.

"Good," Lydia said, "you're aboard. That's the hardest part right there."

Maris exhaled as Lydia let her go. "Good to know."

Though her board drifted a little, the movement was so smooth that she had that strange moment of dislocation when she couldn't tell if it was her moving, or the dock.

Lydia easily got onto her board. "Second safety measure," she said, twisting to reach behind her. She took a velcro strap attached to a coiled rubber rope. "This is called a leash. Put the velcro around your ankle. It'll keep the board with you, in case you fall in."

Maris noted that Ralph already had his on, and followed suit. He smiled and nodded at her.

"Now pick up your paddle," Lydia said, picking up hers. "I've adjusted it to a length that should be good for you, but we can always change it later if you like. Use it like so, to get some distance from the dock." Still kneeling, she and Ralph both used the paddle's wide end, placed it on the wood platform, and slowly pushed away.

Although Maris's paddle landed with a thunk on the wood, she managed to give it a normal push and her paddleboard simply glided away. For a moment she remained still, but found that it didn't rock or feel like it was going to slide out from under her.

"You're doing great," Ralph said. It seemed like he had his paddle at the ready, but was waiting for Lydia's next instructions.

She really ought to hire him, Maris thought, and smiled back. "Thanks."

"And now," Lydia said, "just a few strokes while we're kneeling." She nodded to Ralph.

As she and Maris watched, he carved into the water with the paddle, and pulled—once on the right, and then the left.

Maris glanced at Lydia, who said, "Give it a try."

Imitating Ralph, she did just the same. While he'd made it look effortless, Maris found she had to pull fairly hard, but she managed to get some forward motion. She came up alongside Ralph.

Lydia quickly appeared on her other side, at a distance of a few feet. "A few more strokes," she said, "and then we'll stand."

Ralph paddled forward, and Maris followed him and grinned. She was actually out on the bay.

"To stand," Lydia said from behind her, "put the paddle across the board and keep your hands on it." Ralph followed her directions. He bent forward, laying his paddle across the board and looking as though he was going to crawl forward. "Then, slowly put your feet where your knees are, one at a time, and stand."

Ralph brought one foot forward, followed by the next, and stood, bringing the paddle up with him. He put the wide end in the water and turned his board to see her.

Again, Maris simply tried to do as he did, but once again she'd moved too fast. As she came upright, she started to teeter back.

"Use the paddle," Ralph said quickly.

Maris stuck it in the water, and pulled, righting herself.

"Great," Lydia called out from behind. "We're paddleboarding."

"Now the other side," Ralph encouraged her. "Back and forth, nice and easy."

Maris quickly obeyed and was amazed at the feeling. It had to be like a cross between poling a raft and canoeing. But the extra benefit was being able to stand. She was exhilarated and relieved, all at the same time.

"It's like walking on water," she called out to Lydia and laughed out loud. "Incredible!"

Lydia beamed back at her. "I knew you'd like it."

"The bay really is the perfect place to learn," Ralph said, easily paddling. "The water is so calm right now. So different than this morning."

Maris nodded. "It really is. Like glass."

As she moved forward, Maris took a moment to appreciate her surroundings. The fresh scent of the salt water filled her nostrils, while the brilliant sunlight warmed her skin. The view was incredible, a true 360 degrees, but Maris concentrated on facing forward and keeping her balance.

"These types of all purpose paddleboards are the best for first time users," Lydia said, coming alongside. "They're extremely stable. People bring their kids out on them, and even their pets, sitting right in front."

Maris tried to picture Mojo perched in front of her, and had to smile. "I wonder what Mojo would think."

"People even use them for yoga," Ralph

said. When she looked over to him, he'd set his paddle across the board and had assumed a pose that stretched his back as he reached forward. "It's so peaceful."

Maris had to agree with that. With the exception of their paddles dipping quietly into the water, there was no other sound. Boats tended to steer clear of the lighthouse and the shore. She followed Ralph as the three of them paralleled the sand and rocks. It was wonderful to get this close-up view of the coast, some of which she'd never seen before. Even from the lighthouse, you couldn't see around or over the small hills that jutted out into the water. They formed mini-coves, the first one with its own little beach and a path through the tall grass that led down from the road above.

They travelled south for some time, Lydia and Ralph keeping an eye on her, but also taking in the vistas. The more Maris paddled, the more her timing and coordination improved. She even managed not to think about it for small stretches of time. But before Maris knew it, Ralph slowly turned his paddleboard around in a wide arc.

"Don't want to venture too far on our first time out," he said.

Maris smiled at him. No doubt he and Lydia could have been paddling circles around her this whole time, and still not tired themselves out. But she knew better than to push too hard, particularly at something so new.

"Sounds good," she replied.

The trip back was quicker, perhaps because of the light breeze at their backs, but by the time they reached the dock, Maris found that she was tired, but also relaxed. The prospect of oil drilling on her doorstep and then Audrey's death had been more stress than she'd realized. It'd been good to get away from it all, and simply enjoy what they'd all been fighting to preserve.

Ralph helped her back onto the dock, and Lydia took the paddleboard from the water, piling it on her own.

Maris smiled at them both. "Not only did I learn how to paddleboard, but I gained a new appreciation for this beautiful place. That doesn't happen as often as it should." She beamed at them both. "So thank you. I've enjoyed myself immensely."

Ralph sketched an awkward bow. "Assistant Ralph, at your service."

Lydia laughed and touched Maris's shoulder. "It was wonderful for me too. I adore being able to share my love of the water."

"Well, you certainly accomplished that," Maris agreed, smiling at her. Then she eyed the staircase. "Now we just have to get back up to the B&B."

21

"You looked good out there on the bay," Cookie said, new seedling in one hand and trowel in the other as she took a wide stance in the middle of her garden.

Maris laughed a little. "You could see us?"

Cookie smiled at her. "Until you went down the coast." She bent to the ground and thrust the trowel into the soft soil. "Did you have fun?"

"A ton," Maris said. "It helps when you've got two pros helping you." She gazed back to the water. "It really is a great way to see the bay."

The orange orb of the late afternoon sun was sinking fast, and the sparkling water had turned a rich cobalt blue. As evening enveloped them, the view would change yet again. Despite the amazing stability of the area's weather, no sunset was like another. Each day, each hour, brought a different combination of colors, or simply something that Maris had never really noticed. She shook her head a little. It was ironic that, only on the verge of possibly losing the idyllic scene, was she finally appreciating it.

Even crouching low, Cookie's form cast a long shadow across the many rows of herbs and flowers that she grew. The light sea breeze set some trembling, their tops dancing to an fro, as well as their shadows. The effect was surreal and for a few moments it seemed like the entire garden was gently undulating. Maris paused to take in the aroma as well, the lavender particularly. With a deep breath, she let it fill her lungs and then slowly let it go.

"What are you planting?" she asked.

"Rosemary," the chef replied, pressing down the soil around the little plant. "Transplanting, actually. The seedlings are finally ready for the outdoors." She glanced up at Maris. "Now is the perfect time, so they can settle in without direct sunlight."

"Is rosemary something you'll use in one of your teas or maybe a potion?"

The diminutive chef's magical talent ensured that, whatever ailed you, you'd feel better after sipping one of her creations.

"Actually," she said, standing up. "I'll probably use it for the breakfast potatoes, or maybe to infuse olive oil."

"Ah," Maris said. That was a change. "Something culinary."

Cookie nodded, eying her. "You're looking particularly...relaxed."

Maris smiled at her. "I'm feeling it. Lunch with Mac was wonderful, and the paddleboard was a great way to use some of the calories." She considered for a moment. "Honestly, it's been a perfect day." She left out the fact that there'd been no progress on Audrey's murder, except for Julia's fingerprints on the flyers—which everyone had expected.

Cookie nodded. "Good," she said, and shook the trowel at her. "And it's about time."

Maris laughed a little. Maybe she'd finally been able to tone down her Type A+ behavior. If she could feel like this all the time, she might just bid her overdrive to get things done goodbye. Maybe some things on the to-do list weren't that important after all. She thought back to the fun outing on the bay.

"You know," she said. "I think it might be nice to order some paddleboards for the B&B. They really are pretty simple to use and the safety gear is minimal. We might even win more fans of the bay."

Cookie looked toward the dock, though it wasn't visible from up here. "Store them with the kayaks, then?"

"Yes," Maris answered. "I think we could even stack them."

Cookie moved her gaze back to Maris. "Sounds good." Then she smirked and glanced at the B&B. "I guess Lydia knows how to do her job."

Maris laughed. "Ha! I guess she does." She nodded. "All right, I'll put in the order at the Wine Down." As she turned to head inside to get ready for it, she said, "I'll let you get on with the rosemary while there's still light."

Cookie turned to go back to the greenhouse. "Just a couple more."

22

———

Bright morning sun spilled into the light-filled living room of Millicent Leclair's charming, three-story home.

"Ladies," she said, as she ushered Maris in. "Guess who is joining us today."

Maris had suddenly recalled her precognitive vision of the crochet club when she'd woken up and seen the old photo of Glenda and Cookie on her dressing table. But she'd waited to pay her visit until the usual B&B morning routine had been completed.

"Maris," exclaimed Zarina, smiling. "How wonderful."

Her dark eyes sparkled behind the enormous glasses that she seemed to favor. As usual, she had a headband around her short, dark hair. Likely the same age as Millicent, though quite a bit heavier, the laugh lines and crow's feet etched into her face seem to have been well earned.

"Good to see you, Zarina," Maris said, smiling and nodding to her.

"Come sit," said Vera. She patted the empty chair next to her.

Like Millicent, Vera had elected not to dye her hair. It was completely white, but thick, framing her round face. She wore a small pair of reading glasses perched on the end of her nose, looking over them at Maris.

"Thank you, Vera," Maris said, as she crossed the circle and Millicent resumed her seat near the fireplace.

"It's been a while, young lady," Eunice said. The dour redhead with the frizzy hair and red glasses didn't look up from her project. "That lighthouse must be keeping you busy."

While Vera and Zarina were on the plump side, Eunice was rather thin. If not for the fact that Maris had seen her power walking around the plaza on more than one occasion, she'd have said Eunice looked fragile.

"It's always something, it seems," Maris replied. She reached into her tote bag and brought out her own project—the same one she always brought.

"What have you got there?" Helen asked. She lifted her horn-rimmed glasses a bit for a better look. "Ah, your potholder."

Though the thin older woman wore thick lenses, she was working on a doily with a hook that was so small, Maris couldn't see it from across the circle.

"Yes," she said, holding up the irregular patch of red and ochre yarn. "The never-ending potholder."

"More like hardly begun," Eunice said.

"Now Eunice," Millicent chided. "We all work at our own pace."

Helen nodded at the potholder, and gave Maris a wink. "I still like those colors."

As Maris glanced around the circle, she saw that Zarina was working on a pair of dusty pink baby boots; Vera was crocheting a scarf with thick, sage colored yarn. Of course, Helen with her doily seemed to be crocheting string, but it was a beautiful combination of white, lavender and purple. Eunice was working on something huge that looked to Maris like it might be a cape or a shoulder wrap of some sort. While most of it was crimson, the border was black.

As usual, Millicent had the most colorful project. Maris wondered if the aura reader could see colors that were out of this world, because her yarn choices certainly looked like it. She was crocheting a ski cap that looked like it had every color in the visible and invisible spectrums.

The five other ladies sat quietly, working on their projects, but glancing furtively at one another. Maris knew they were waiting for her to start the conversation and let them know the real reason for her visit.

"The death of Audrey Graisser," Maris said. "Horrible business."

Almost as one, they set their projects in their laps.

"Simply dreadful," Zarina agreed, staring at Maris through the huge spectacles.

Vera nodded and peered over her reading glasses. "Awful. Truly awful."

Helen took off her horn-rimmed glasses. "Such a lovely young girl," she said sadly.

Everyone looked to Millicent. Her twinkling black eyes landed on each of them in turn, settling finally on Maris.

"I take it you were there," the leader of the cabal said.

Though it sounded like a simple statement, Maris knew that the negotiation had begun. Where information was currency, Millicent had just asked for a good faith deposit.

Maris nodded. "I was there, as I'm sure you know." There were prim smiles all around, even from Eunice. They could likely tell her the name of every single person at the rally. "Perhaps you've heard that very little evidence was found near the body, because of the sand."

"No footprints," Millicent agreed.

"Nothing accidentally dropped," Zarina added.

"Except for the flyers," Vera said.

Helen nodded. "I think that sums it up."

"Well," Maris began slowly, "it turns out the flyers had fingerprints on them." Everyone leaned forward a bit, even Millicent. "Those of Julia Mendes."

A quick look shot around the circle, as they all sat back.

"Naturally," Millicent finally said. "That makes sense."

Everyone went back to their projects, and Maris even managed to crochet a few links that were the same size. After enough time had passed, she said, "Naturally you've also heard that the fishing spear that killed her was taken from Castaways." There was no acknowledgement, but all work stopped, even if they didn't lift their gazes. "Ryan Quigg," Maris continued, as though she was idly musing. "A very nice young man, avid fisherman, and..." She glanced at Millicent. "...if I had to guess, I'd say he might be one of the magic folk."

Again, all eyes landed on Millicent, who nodded to Eunice.

The redhead put down her cape, and looked directly at Maris. "He is," she declared.

Although Maris was glad for the confirmation, Pixie Point Bay etiquette prevented her from asking exactly what his talent might be. Apparently, Millicent understood her predicament.

"You might say," the club president said, "that we've put together a few clues over time." She glanced at Zarina, who smiled, her cheeks lifting the large glasses.

"When there's even a hint of humidity in the air," she said, "there's a rainbow over his shop."

Maris's eyebrows went up.

"Curious," said Vera, looking over the glasses on the end of her nose. "A shop that never seems to earn much money and yet doesn't have finance worries."

"Ever seen him fish in the early morning twilight?" Helen asked. "It seems like the light is playing a trick on old eyes, but it just might be that those fishing rods of his have a bit of sparkle to them."

"I'm telling you," Eunice said, scowling at Millicent. "He's got a pot of gold in there."

Maris frowned a little. A rainbow, a sparkling rod, and a pot of gold? It started to ring a bell. The young Mr. Quigg was of Irish descent. She sat back in her chair as the pieces finally fit together: Ryan was a leprechaun. When she looked at Millicent, the old woman was watching her with a knowing look on her face. She simply nodded.

All those times on the pier that Maris had seen him reeling in one fish after another...

He'd imbued his rod and reel with the luck of the Irish.

Once again the ladies picked up their projects, as did Maris. As their conversation turned to Zarina's new great-grandchild, and then Helen's home needing a new roof, Maris wasn't really listening.

If Ryan could cast some luck on his tackle, had he also done that to the spear gun?

It had to be an unwieldy weapon at the best of times, let alone on land. Yet it had been successfully used to kill someone.

Maris had hoped that her visit to the club would yield new information—which it had done—but it had also pointed her in a direction of which she wasn't too fond. By the time she returned her attention to her project, she found she'd begun to make her potholder rectangular instead of square. As she tugged on the yarn, undoing the last few rows, she sighed. It was like her investigation, seeming to get somewhere and then unraveling.

23

Although Maris wasn't surprised to see Julia Mendes' car in front of the B&B, she was shocked to see what the young woman was doing. At the back of the building, in Cookie's herb garden, she was using a trowel to move some soil into a hole. Cookie stood on the other side of the row of plants, pointing down at it, as Bear brought over a big bag of compost.

"Good afternoon, you three," Maris said, as she joined them.

Julia looked up at her from where she knelt, hands still in the dirt, smiling. "Hey, Maris."

She put her hands on her hips. "It looks like Cookie's found a way to put you to work too."

Cookie opened her mouth to make a reply, but Julia laughed. "Oh no," the young woman said. "I pretty much forced my way in here."

"Nonsense," the diminutive chef told her. "I'm always glad for the help."

Bear set the bag down and looked at Maris. "I have the electrical parts in the truck."

She held up her hand. "I see you're needed out here. There's no hurry on the electricity. It turns out I don't miss it as much as I thought I would."

Cookie handed Julia another seedling.

"Basil," the young woman said grinning. "Oh, I adore this on pizza." She stroked one of the leaves. "And the shape is so pretty too."

Maris regarded her. "You know your plants."

Julia sat back on her heels and looked around at the rows of flowers and herbs. "Gardening is how I got my start in environmentalism. I've gardened since I was four. It completely captivated me, putting a seed in the soil and then seeing the first green shoot."

Cookie patted her on the shoulder. "I know how you feel."

As Julia looked up at the chef, she also cast her gaze out to the bay. "Of all the places I've been in the world, I've never seen a spot that's blessed by so many of the right elements." She looked up at the lighthouse, and then at the house, glancing at Maris. "Not to mention the picturesque lighthouse and lightkeeper's house."

Maris smiled at her. "I couldn't agree more."

For several moments the four of them simply stood and took in the view. But as Maris let her gaze drift up to the optical room at the top of the lighthouse, she had an idea.

"Speaking of the lighthouse," she said, "I've got to check on something." She exchanged a look with Cookie. "I'll let you get back to it."

Cookie nodded to her, and Maris headed toward the Old Girl. Before Claribel could open the door for her, Maris hurried forward, catching the knob just as a swirling sea breeze blew it open.

"Thanks," she said quietly, as she slipped inside and closed the door behind her.

Like the generations of lightkeepers before her, Maris had a special bond with the magical lighthouse. As she climbed the spiral, wrought iron staircase, she imagined her aunt climbing these very same stairs, perhaps for the very same purpose. Glenda had never told her about the family's magic abilities or the remote viewing that Claribel provided. It had been Cookie who'd clued her in.

From the window of the second story, a shaft of sunlight sliced across the interior of the tower. The spotlight it created was almost too bright to look at. As her course spiraled upward, she imagined the blazing rectangle tracing an arc across the interior during the course of the day. When she mounted the third story, it occurred to her that the windows on the different levels would each trace their own arc at different times of day as the sun came through them in turn. It would be like a lovely dance of light, albeit a slow one.

Breathing hard—though not as hard as she had when she first returned—Maris took a final step onto the metal grating that served as the floor of the glass room at the top. She never tired of this view but today she simply looked down on the bay. Perhaps it was the slant of the sun, or maybe the time of year, but she'd never seen the shifting colors of turquoise and sapphire so clearly in the water just below. It was subtle but definitely there, starting with the lightest blue near the rocky shore and transitioning to the darker color as the water got deeper. Maris found herself smiling at it but quickly turned to the heart of the light beam behind her, the fresnel lens. She had come here on urgent business.

There had to be nearly one hundred pieces of sculpted and etched pieces of glass, each one crystal clear. They were held in place by a sturdy steel frame that stood a bit taller than her, since the base of it rested on the mechanism that turned it.

As she'd learned to do, Maris relaxed her neck and shoulders, and let her mind go empty. With an unfocused gaze, she looked into the base of the lens. Tiny rainbows danced within it, refracting the sunlight. As she watched, they seemed to swirl and drift until a vision swam into view.

"Flour Power," she whispered.

As though she were looking through a telescope, she saw the gas station and sandwich shop run by Jude and Fab Toussaint. Everything there appeared normal: someone was getting gas at one of the station's two pumps; Jude was wiping his hands on a rag as he moved around inside the repair bay; an older couple looked as though they'd just bought sandwiches. Maris frowned at it a little, and then it winked out.

"Hmm," she muttered. Though she couldn't see a connection with the murder of Audrey Graisser, she knew better than to question the Old Girl. Instead she gently patted the base. "Thank you, Claribel."

As she descended the spiral staircase, she tried to remember if she needed any work done on her car, or maybe an oil change. The used car that Jude had arranged for her was running like a top. She shrugged. At the very least, she could buy gas.

On the ground floor, she'd just been about to open the door, when she heard someone shouting beyond it.

24

O utside the tower, Maris immediately saw and heard the source of the loud voice. Joseph Toler was bellowing at the top of his lungs from the edge of the garden. As Maris rushed over, Julia hid behind Bear while Cookie pointed at the plants just in front of the irate lawyer.

"Don't step on those," she said.

Maris approached Toler. "What's going on here?"

He wheeled on her, and shook a piece of paper in her face. "Someone left this on my bed!"

She quickly recognized one of the flyers from the rally. "It's just–"

Toler quickly flipped it around to show

her the back. Someone had printed some-thing in big letters. Though she could read it, the lawyer read it out loud. "Leave or you'll suffer the same fate as Audrey." He shook it at Julia. "And the fishhook in the corner? Nice touch."

Though Maris hadn't seen it at first, the barbed piece of metal was stuck through the paper at the bottom. A short piece of frayed and dirty fishing line dangled from it.

"This is unacceptable," the lawyer de-clared, and hurled the flyer at the ground. He took his cell phone from his pocket. "And I'm not going to sit still for it."

As he dialed a number, Maris exchanged a look with Cookie, who only shrugged.

"I didn't put that there," Julia said, her voice small and shaking. "I don't know any-thing about it."

Bear glanced over his shoulder at her, be-fore returning his attention to Toler.

"Sheriff?" the man said into his phone. "This is Joseph Toler. I've just received a threatening letter on my bed here at the B&B." He glared at Julia and then Maris, then seemed to listen to something Mac was say-ing. "Come and see for yourself," he yelled. "I don't know what kind of rinky-dink investigation you're running, but I want some answers and now also protection." He turned away and started to stalk back to the house. "I want you here ASAP." There was another pause before he went through the back door. But from the interior they could hear more shouting. "I don't care!" The rest was indistinct.

Cookie went to the flyer and bent to pick it up.

"Don't," Maris cautioned her, and the chef stopped in mid-reach. "That's evidence now." She looked at Bear and Julia. "No one touch it. Mac will have to collect it."

25

As Maris led Mac through the house, she said, "It's in the garden, where he dropped it. No one has touched it."

He already had glove and evidence bag in hand. "Good," he said, as they approached the garden where Cookie waited. He glanced around. "Where are Mr. Toler and Ms. Mendes?"

"Joseph left first," Maris told him. "He stormed off right after he showed us the flyer." Maris pointed to it, at Cookie's feet.

"Standing guard?" Mac asked her.

"We didn't want to take a chance that it'd blow away," she said to him.

"Good thinking," he said as he snapped on the glove.

"Julia left not long after Joseph," Maris continued. "They were both upset."

"Julia was afraid," Cookie added. "I think that much was clear."

Mac looked up at her. "Of Toler?"

The chef nodded. "Thank goodness Bear was here. The lawyer was in a rage."

Mac opened the evidence bag, carefully picked up the flyer, and put it inside. He examined the ground for a few moments, before standing up. Then he sealed the bag and removed the glove.

He glanced between Maris and Cookie. "What did Bear do?"

Cookie smirked a little. "Absolutely nothing."

The sheriff's eyebrows rose a little. He gave Maris an inquiring look.

"That's exactly right," she said. "He simply stood right there." She pointed to where his big boot prints were still in the soil. "Julia hid behind him."

"I see," the sheriff said, his face stern as he apparently pictured the scene. "And you say both of them left?" Maris nodded. "Did they leave their luggage?"

"I'm pretty sure they did, but we can check."

Mac turned to the chef. "Thanks for your help, Cookie."

She smiled at him. "I'm happy to stand in my garden any time."

Back inside the house, Maris and Mac climbed the stairs together.

"The barnacle analysis came back," he said. "It's the same species as found under the pier. As small a piece of data as that may be, it's at least a bit of evidence."

They mounted to the second floor. "Right," Maris agreed. He looked around at the different rooms and Maris pointed at Julia's. "You just want to make sure they haven't left?"

The sheriff nodded. "Judging from your description of the events, and what I heard on the phone, I can see why they'd both want to leave. The sooner I know that they've left, the sooner I can put out a bulletin."

But as they looked in on both rooms, the luggage was where it usually was. If they'd fled, they hadn't taken their belongings.

"Good," Mac said. He looked at the flyer

and the scrawled message on the back. "Obviously I'll have it fingerprinted, but I'll also be getting some writing samples. I'm not sure there's anything we can do with the hook."

As they went back downstairs, Maris said, "I have the guests fill out a card to get the make and model of their vehicles when they arrive. I'll get those together for you."

"Great," the sheriff said, and checked his watch. "But I'll have to get those from you later." He hefted the evidence bag. "I want to get this to the lab right away." They went to the front door, which he opened.

"I'll text you when I have the information," she said.

He paused on the front porch, and gave her a little smile. "I had a nice time at lunch yesterday."

She grinned back at him, and felt a flush of heat in her cheeks. "Me too."

He nodded quickly. "Good," he said. Then glanced at the flyer. "Good," he said again, and then turned and headed to his vehicle.

Although Maris would have waited and given him a goodbye wave, she heard footsteps behind her.

"Maris?" Bear said.

"Yes, Bear," she said, closing the door.

"Can I show you the fuse box?"

26

In the utility room, Maris stood back as Bear opened the metal door of the fuse box. But when Maris peered inside, she hardly recognized it. It was clean and clearly labelled, but all the fuse switches looked the same.

"I don't understand," she said. "Where's the new fuse?"

For a moment, he looked perplexed, and glanced between her and the fuse box. Then he smiled at her. "All of them are new."

She cocked her head back as her mouth dropped open. "What?"

Bear's brows drew together in a bit of worry. "I replaced them all?"

"But why?" She stopped for a moment and held up a hand. "What I mean to say is that's wonderful. But I thought I only ruined the one."

"You didn't ruin it," Bear said.

Maris frowned a bit. "Okay, now you've lost me. I turned on my new hair dryer and fried the fuse. It's just too powerful."

Bear shook his head. "Your hair dryer didn't do it." He nodded back toward the bedroom. "You can try it."

Maris hesitated. "Are you...sure?" She'd hate to see all his hard work go to waste.

He smiled and nodded. "Yes."

She took a deep breath. "If you're sure..."

In the bathroom, she was reaching for the dryer on the shelf when she looked into the sink and shrieked. It was a squirrel. She jumped back.

Bear was there in a flash. "What is it?" he said, his giant frame filling the door.

"In the sink," she said pointing. "A squirrel. I don't know how it got in here."

Bear squeezed past her and looked down into the basin. He reached his big hand in.

"Be careful," Maris urged. "It might bite."

"Not this one," he said, and brought it out.

"Oh no," she muttered. "Is it dead?"

Bear turned to her and held it out. "You could say that."

Although she recoiled a little, she could finally see it clearly. "A toy?" She exhaled with relief and put a hand to her chest. "Mojo. It has to be one of his."

Bear tried to stand back as far as he could. "Do you want to plug in the hair dryer?"

"Right," she said, having forgotten the reason she'd come in. She took it from the shelf, made sure it was switched off, then plugged it in. In the mirror, Bear encouraged her with a waggle of his eyebrows. "Okay," she said. "Here we go."

She thumbed it on—and almost jumped when it fired right up. For a few seconds she waited for it to stop, but it kept running. On impulse, she flipped on the light switch too. Overhead, the light came on. Bear grinned at her from the mirror, and she turned off the hair dryer.

"It works," she exclaimed, grinning back at him, until she realized she had him trapped by the shower. "Here," she said, unplugging the appliance and putting it on the shelf. She went into the bedroom and then the utility room, and took another look at the fuse box.

"But why replace them all?" she said turning to the brawny handyman.

"Because they were all the same age. They only last about thirty years."

Maris glanced in the direction of the bathroom. "So you're saying it wasn't the hair dryer, it was the fuse itself."

Bear nodded. "It got old. They all had. So it was time to replace them."

She looked from him back to the panel, and then back to him again, as she smirked. "You're a genius."

The cheeks above his beard turned a bright pink and he shrugged. "It was maintenance. Really simple."

Perhaps it'd only been natural for her to jump to the conclusion about the hair dryer, but Bear was right. It'd simply been a matter of noticing the obvious.

Maris frowned. Noticing the obvious. She thought of the flyers under the pier. There was something obvious there, something she wasn't seeing.

Bear picked up his tool bag. "I'll see if Cookie needs any help."

"Thank you, Bear. This is really wonderful work. We're awfully lucky to have you."

He only ducked his head, and then hurried from the room.

As Maris closed the door on the fuse box, she pictured the flyers on the sand. Bear had spotted the obvious, and now...

"Wait a minute," she muttered, gripping the door. "That's it. It has to be."

Quickly she closed it, grabbed her purse, and headed to the front door.

27

Even from the driveway of Flour Power Sandwiches & Gas Station, Maris spotted Julia's car parked outside the shop. Claribel had, of course, been right.

Although she did need gas and an oil check before she left, Maris pulled up next to Julia's car. Inside, the young woman was sitting at one of the high tables staring down into a cup of coffee.

"Maris," Fab said. "Good to see you."

Fabiola Toussaint and her husband had fled from Haiti before landing in Pixie Point Bay. Maris was sure that if the woman had been born in New York or Paris, she'd have been a super model. Tall, thin, and graceful, her chocolate skin was flawless and glowed with that golden energy of youth. Behind her shoulders, her dark hair fell straight down, all the way to her waist.

"Sandwich for you today?" she asked, smiling her gorgeous smile. "Or maybe a croissant?"

Although Maris had been looking into the display case at the baked goods, she shook her head. "No, thank you," she replied wistfully. "But I'd adore one of your tasty lattes with low fat milk." She took the appropriate cash from her wallet and slid it across the counter. "Keep the change."

Fab rang up the purchase on the register. "One latte, coming right up."

Although Julia must have heard Fab say Maris's name, she pointedly stared down into her cup. Of course, Maris wasn't so easily put off. She strode over to the table and placed a hand on the back of the empty chair opposite her.

"Mind if I join you?" she asked, smiling.

Hands around her cup, Julia sighed heavily and never looked up. "Suit yourself."

"Thank you," Maris said, pulling out the chair and taking a seat. Although she waited for a few moments, Julia said nothing. "The coffee here is wonderful, don't you think? But don't tell Cookie I was here." At that, Julia looked up. Maris dropped her voice a notch. "She's been trying to wean me off caffeine since I arrived." She arched her eyebrows. "She thinks she has."

Julia had to smile a little. "Your secret is safe."

Maris settled back into the chair. "The sheriff came and collected the flyer from the garden." She paused for a moment. "I'm sorry about that business with Joseph."

"Me too," she said quietly.

Fab came over and deposited the latte on the table. A coffee colored heart was swirled into the foam. On the saucer was a small, round sugar cookie. Maris grinned at her. "Beautiful. Thank you."

"My pleasure," Fab said. She turned to Julia. "Would you like a refill?"

The young woman shook her head. "No, I'm good. Thanks."

Fab nodded to them both. "Enjoy."

Maris took a sip and set the cup down, warming her hands around it. "Oh, that is good."

Julia took a sip of her coffee too.

"The sheriff will probably have the fingerprints rushed," Maris said.

Julia grimaced. "Of course it'll have my prints all over it," she grumbled. "They all have my fingerprints. I distributed them."

"Exactly," Maris agreed. "The one in Joseph's room. The ones under the pier." Though Maris now had her suspicions of how they'd gotten down there, she would have to approach this carefully.

But before she could begin, Julia covered her face with trembling hands. "I can't believe this," she said, and began to cry.

Maris got up and went to the small table with the sugar, creamer, and napkins, and grabbed a handful. Fab looked on with concern and sympathy, but Maris motioned with her hand that it was under control. When she came back to the table, Julia was shaking her head. Maris handed her a napkin, and the young woman took it and wiped her nose.

"I swore I'd never get myself into a situation like this," Julia said.

Maris cocked an eyebrow at her. "A situation like a murder?"

Julia blew her nose and then shook her

head, the tears still falling. "No," she managed to say. "Being a victim."

Maris's eyebrows flew up. "A victim? In what way?"

Julia finally looked at her. Even through the pooling tears, there was something deeply determined in her gaze. "I'll tell you why I've devoted my life to environmental activism. Because of my cousin. He's the one who taught me to garden when I was a child. He was the one who instilled a reverence for nature in me, who made sure I got tuition money when I needed it."

Maris smiled at her. "He sounds incredible."

"He *was*," Julia said, her voice breaking. "He was an environmental activist too, but he became a victim. He died in a whale-hunting intervention. He..." She burst into a sob.

Maris pushed the rest of the napkins toward her. "I'm so sorry." The young woman only took another napkin and blew her nose again. "Look, Julia," Maris said quietly. "I think I can help you. I know you're scared, and for good reason. But unless you tell me everything, there's nothing that I can do." The young woman glanced at her, wiping her nose. "If you can help me, then I'm sure we can get all of this sorted out. And I swear to you that you will not be a victim. But you've got to tell me what happened. Can you do that?"

Julia took a shaky breath, but sat up taller. Finally she nodded. "I will. I'll do it for my cousin. For Xavier."

OUTSIDE THE SANDWICH SHOP, once Julia had driven off, Maris got in her car. She took out her cell and dialed Mac's number. Just from the sound of his voice, she could tell he was smiling.

"Maris," he said, in that beautiful baritone. "How nice to hear from you."

She smiled in return. "You'll really think so once I tell you about the murder weapon."

There was a sound on the other end of the phone as though he was switching it between ears. "What have you got?"

"I think you're going to find the actual spear gun in the surf under the pier," she said quickly.

"In the surf," he said. There was a pause.

"I don't suppose you care to tell me how you know."

"Not as yet," she said. "I want to make sure it's there first."

"Making sure," he said, not sounding too happy.

Although he couldn't see her, she shrugged. "I don't want to start pointing fingers until you can find the gun and see if it has fingerprints."

"Fingerprints?" he said. "Assuming we can even find it, it's been in saltwater." He paused. "Although..."

Maris waited for a few moments, as though he might elaborate. When he didn't she said, "Although?"

"All right," he answered. "It's at least worth a couple of scuba divers and metal detectors."

"Search the water just north of where the body was found," she suggested. "That's everything I can tell you."

"It's good enough to start," he said. "Not to cut this short, but this is going to be time critical. I'll need to get on it right away."

"Good luck," she said.

28

Because Jude had recommended an oil change, the trip to the gas station had taken Maris longer than she'd planned. Even so, the Wine Down was still a couple of hours away, so she decided on a little detour into town. Ever since her internet research into oil derrick technology, she'd been bothered. After she parked outside the Main Street Market and got out, she paused and gave her temple a discreet tap to quickly review what she'd seen.

With a nod, she shouldered her purse and went inside. Howard had been rummaging for something under the counter behind the antique register, but stood up when he heard the bell on the door.

"Maris," he said smiling. "Two shopping

sprees in a week. Business must be brisk at the B&B."

"It's about average," she said, moving to the counter. Though she smiled back, she picked up one of his flyers. "I was curious about this diagram of yours." She tapped on it. "So I decided to educate myself."

"Oh really?" he said, grinning. The ends of his mustache lifted, and the surrounding laugh lines deepened. "That's good to hear."

"The internet is an amazing collection of information," she said, starting slowly. "I'd never heard of air guns used to drill for oil. I was reading about how they can ruin an ecosystem." He nodded vigorously in agreement. "And then one click led to another, since I'm not familiar with any of the science terminology."

"All you have to do is ask," he said. "I'll try not to use my professor voice."

She smiled, but continued. "I eventually tracked it all down." She paused, looking down at the flyer. "But it turns out the internet is also a bit of a time machine. There I was, just clicking around, and I came across a patent by a certain young physicist."

Howard's smile vanished. For a few awkward moments he simply stared at her, and then he frowned. "I see," he said. "I'd wondered." Then he sighed. "But I never managed to find it myself." His big dark eyes looked directly into hers. "I never imagined it would be used for oil drilling. I tried to stop it, too." He shook his head. "But you can't unring the bell. Not a day goes by that I don't regret putting that technology out there."

Maris shook her head. "If it hadn't been you, wouldn't it have been someone else?"

He shrugged. "Who knows?" He picked up a flyer from the counter between them. "What I do know is that I played a part in it. And now?" He showed her the piece of paper. "Now I'm doing everything that I can to right that wrong."

"But you couldn't have known how it'd be used," she protested.

"Maybe yes, maybe no," he said, and put the flyer down. "But what's in the past is done. All that anyone can do in the present is what they think is right."

There was no arguing with that. "Your logic is impeccable," she said, with a little smile. "And I'm totally with you on advocating against the NAP oil derrick." She set her flyer down on his in the stack. "It's not important where that particular technology came from. No one needs to know." She nodded at him. "As you say, all we can do is look to the future. Work for a brighter one."

He finally smiled. "I couldn't agree more."

She glanced at her watch. It was time to head home. But Howard moved to the glass candy jars and used a tissue to fetch her favorite. He hurried back and offered it to her. "A barber pole for the little lady?"

She grinned at him as she took it. Despite the rally and the flyers and his anger at a past mistake, he was the same Howard she'd always known. "Thank you. I'll see you next time."

29

In the darkness of early morning, Maris reached to the Tiffany lamp on the nightstand and pulled on the chain. Despite the hour and the blaring of her phone, her first thought was about how glad she was to have electricity. Had Bear not replaced the fuses, she'd be rushing to throw on her robe and find her phone elsewhere. Instead, she picked it up from its charger and saw who was calling. As Mojo raised his head to stare at it, she sat up and hit the answer button.

"Mac," she said, her voice rough. She cleared her throat. "I hope this means you've got good news."

"Apologies for the early hour," he said, "but yes. That's exactly why I'm calling."

For a few minutes he described the details of his findings, and concluded, "I had to spend a few brownie points, and I'll owe some favors, but this will close the case." Mojo got up, draped his front paws over her lap, and gave her his signature meow. She heard Mac laugh. "Tell Mojo that, in the words of the great philosopher, 'Instant gratification isn't soon enough.'"

Maris frowned a little. "Is that Burns?"

"Carrie Fisher," he answered.

Maris laughed as she stroked the little cat's head and back. "When will you be here?"

"I can make it in half an hour," he replied, "but I doubt that anyone is up but you."

"Oh, I imagine Cookie is up," she said. "But you're right about the guests. Let's make it after breakfast, and I'll ask Joseph and Julia to stay until you arrive. Say 10:30?"

"I'll see you then," he said.

"See you then," she said, and hung up.

As she continued to pet a very contented looking Mojo, she had to smile. "It's finally over," she whispered.

30

I n the living room of the B&B, with the fog outside just clearing, everyone had gathered. Julia sat on the cushions of the bay window that looked out toward the front of the house. Joseph sat as far away from her as possible, near the door that led to the library. As the townspeople who'd helped Julia to clean up after the rally—and also fallen under suspicion—Maris had also invited Ryan and Howard, who sat together on the couch. Mac stood at the hallway entrance to the room, while Maris stood opposite him, in front of the fireplace.

It hadn't escaped her notice that the B&B's two other guests, Ralph and Lydia, were lingering with their coffee in the dining room. Though they were out of sight, they could no doubt easily hear the little gathering. For all Maris knew, Ralph might actually be live-blogging what he heard.

"Thank you all for coming," she said, looking around at the rough circle. "I know some of us have businesses to operate at this time of day." She glanced at Ryan and Howard, but let her gaze linger on the market owner. "But all of us were at the rally the day that Audrey was killed," she said to him. "And all of us had our own reasons for being there."

Howard held his head high and met her gaze. "I want to take this opportunity to thank you for the work you've done to investigate her death, and for asking me here. But also..." He paused and swallowed, glancing at Ryan. "I know only too well the risks associated with an oil derrick, particularly the drilling operation." He looked at Julia. "Early in my science career, United Oil made use of a technology that I pioneered, to disastrous ends." The young woman gasped a little as she stared at him. "It's not something I'm proud of." He turned to look at Maris. "But it's the reason I'll do whatever it takes to make sure oil drilling doesn't come to Pixie Point Bay. I'm willing to gather the data, write the reports, and testify. I am at your disposal."

"Thank you, Howard," she said smiling at him. As he nodded and smiled back at her, she watched as his shoulders lifted and the lines in his forehead eased. "We may yet need that."

Her gaze fell on Ryan, who sat next to him. "We know the murder weapon came from your shop, Ryan." Though the young man looked at her, he remained silent. "But what I'd like you to tell the sheriff is when it disappeared." He glanced at Julia, frowned, and glared back at her. "It's all right," she said gently. "Just tell the truth."

He grimaced a little, but looked up at Mac. "It disappeared the day that Julia dropped off flyers in my shop."

"I didn't take it," she protested.

"I didn't say that," Ryan quickly added. "I think Julia is doing an absolutely great job."

Mac held up a hand. "No one said Julia took it." He glanced at Joseph. "Ms. Mendes arrived in town the same day that Ms.

Graisser and Mr. Toler did. They were canvasing the Towne Plaza, same as her."

The lawyer scowled at him, and then Maris. "I'd like to remind you two that Ms. Mendes gets paid to do her job, like anybody else. She's no environmental saint." He looked at Ryan and Howard. "It's naive in the extreme to assume she's here out of the goodness of her heart. In fact, it's naive to think an oil derrick won't be placed in the bay. If not NAP, who has an impeccable record, then maybe a company like United Oil." He pointedly looked at Howard, before pointing a finger at Julia. "Only one person in this room stood to gain from my colleague's death—or even mine." Now he glared at Ryan. "I'm the one who received the death threat. I wonder where that hook came from?" He fixed his gaze on Julia. "I wonder if the two of you aren't working together."

Although Ryan opened his mouth, Maris cut him off. "Speaking of that note," she said loudly. "I was there when you brought it to the garden." She tilted her head at the young environmentalist. "Julia had to hide behind Bear. She was obviously afraid." She crossed her arms over her chest. "But why hide behind Bear?" She looked at the lawyer. "Did she really think you'd do something in front of us?" When he made to answer, she stopped him. "The answer was obvious. I just didn't see it. For example, the obvious answer as to how the flyers ended up under the pier is that Julia was there."

Ryan took in a sharp breath, and whipped his head around to look at the young woman. Her shoulders hunched and she seemed to cave in on herself. "It's true," she said in a trembling voice. "I was there."

"What?" Howard said. He shot a glance at Maris, then turned back to Julia. "I don't believe it."

Julia hugged herself around the middle. "Believe me," she said. "I wish it wasn't true. But it is." She looked between Ryan and Howard. "I didn't kill Audrey, but..." She looked at Mac. "I saw who did."

"You saw it?" Howard said, incredulous. "You saw who killed her? But why didn't you say so?"

"Because...because I was afraid for my life," she whispered, staring at the floor. "My cousin was killed in a whale hunting intervention, on purpose. It's something that's haunted me ever since."

"Well then, who killed her?" Ryan asked.

Julia raised her gaze and leveled it at Joseph.

The lawyer jumped up from his seat and took a step in her direction. "That's ridiculous. I would never–"

Mac crossed the room in two long strides. He put a hand on Toler's shoulder. "Please have a seat, Mr. Toler."

"But I–" he protested.

Mac tightened his grip and came between him and the rest of the room. "Please have a seat. I won't ask a second time."

Though Toler's red face glared at him, he finally took a step back and Mac let him go. As the lawyer sat back down, Mac stood next to him but turned back to the room.

"That was why you hid behind Bear," Maris said to Julia. "You were afraid for your life, but not because of what happened in the garden." The young woman nodded. "Tell us what you saw."

"I was picking up flyers from the sand, when I heard raised voices." She looked at Mac. "I was behind one of the pier's pillars when I saw them. Joseph and Audrey that is. They were arguing."

"This is insane," Toler grumbled.

"Let her finish," Mac told him.

Although the lawyer angrily crossed his arms over his chest, he remained silent.

"What were they arguing about?" Maris asked.

"The emails about the EIRs and how they'd been done by companies with ties to NAP. She was livid at being blindsided, and wanted to know what was going on." She finally looked at Toler. "You called her a liability. Then she threatened to get you fired. When you brought out the spear gun you told her she was only worth drumming up sympathy, and worth way more than killing 'the activist', though I was next on the list." She looked at Maris. "In the end, Audrey begged for her life. She was trying to run when he shot her. Then he hurled the gun into the ocean."

Ryan looked at Toler. "I did speak to Audrey that day—the day Julia dropped off the flyers. We were on the sidewalk. But you..." He cast a sideways glance to the floor, before returning his gaze to the lawyer. "Where were you? In the shop?"

Mac looked down at the man, who had begun to look nervous. "It turns out that Mr. Toler has a fishing license."

Toler scoffed and looked up at him. "Which only makes me a law-abiding citizen."

"Except that on your social media accounts," the sheriff calmly replied, "your type of fishing seems to be snorkeling and spear fishing."

Now Toler forced a laugh. "Social media doesn't prove anything. It's my word against hers, and I'm an officer of the court."

Mac nodded to Maris, who went behind the couch and picked up a large evidence bag. Julia gasped when she saw it. Easily seen through the clear plastic was a spear gun. She handed it to Mac.

"That's the one that went missing," Ryan confirmed.

The sheriff nodded. "It was right where Julia said it would be."

Toler pointed at her. "Because it was right where she threw it."

Mac grinned at the lawyer. "I've had it fingerprinted."

Ryan gaped at the weapon. "But it was in the ocean, in the surf."

The sheriff nodded. "Latent fingerprints. Still there." He looked at Maris. "It's a process called the superglue technique."

"A small particle reagent," Howard added. "Yes, combined with cyanoacrylate fuming." Ryan arched his eyebrows at the storekeeper. "The chemicals in superglue react with the oils, fats, and proteins in the skin." He rubbed his fingers together. "The superglue turns white, and you get a white fingerprint."

"And they're yours, Mr. Toler," the sheriff said. "Matching up nicely with those found on the flyer with the fish hook."

"Right," Maris said. "The threatening letter that you wrote yourself."

Suddenly she remembered Mojo's tarot card, the six of pentacles and the man holding the scales. They represented the legal profession, not riches.

"Did you also put the barnacle in her room?" Maris asked, but Toler made no reply.

"Reprehensible," Howard muttered. His

dark eyes seemed to burn into Toler's who looked away. "And yet how predictable that you and NAP would use the murder of your own liaison to generate support."

"You can stand now, Mr. Toler," Mac said, withdrawing the handcuffs from his belt. "You're under arrest for the murder of Audrey Graisser."

31

At the end of the dock, Maris watched Ralph and Lydia get the paddleboards ready. As soon as Mac had taken Toler into custody, the living room gathering had broken up. Howard and Ryan had hurried off to return to their businesses. Although Julia had been grateful for what Maris had done, she packed and left as well, apparently anxious to put the whole thing behind her.

Only the travel blogger and traveling salesman remained, though today would be their last day.

"Are you sure you won't join us?" Ralph asked Maris. "It's shaping up to be another beautiful day."

"We're going to head north this time," Lydia said, hooking up her ankle line. "Toward the pier."

Maris toasted them with her cup of tea. "I'll enjoy watching you. I need to get caught up on a few things."

Ralph stood on his board and dipped his paddle in the water. "NAP stock took a huge tumble this morning. It appears that news of Toler's arrest has leaked out—somehow." He smiled impishly. "There's even speculation that NAP knew about Audrey, maybe even ordered it."

Lydia stood too. "Well, I'm just glad he'll be brought to justice." She gazed out at the water. "And even gladder that the bay will be preserved." She glanced back at Ralph. "Ready?"

"Absolutely," he said and began to paddle. But as they departed, he looked back over his shoulder. "By the way, you might want to prepare for a glut of new visitors. I've been raving on my blog about how magical your lighthouse and B&B are. Cheers!"

"Thanks," Maris called out to him, and gave them a wave.

As they paddled out, her gaze followed them and she had to grin. Ralph had summed it up nicely, and she decided she couldn't agree more if she tried.

The Witch Who Heard the Music

Excerpt

CHAPTER ONE

If Maris Seaver hadn't known she was standing in the Towne Plaza of Pixie Point Bay, she'd never have recognized it. The normally tranquil scene and a throwback to a bygone era had transformed into a bustling maelstrom of activity. Excitement buzzed in the air like cicadas in summer.

"It's amazing, isn't it?" said a familiar voice.

Maris had parked in front of the Main Street Market, but it wasn't Howard that greeted her. It was Helen Tellur, a member of the crochet club, By Hook or Crook. It was located next to the general store and looked out on the Towne Plaza—and its members had to be thrilled. There was no end to the action or people that the busiest busy-bodies in the world could watch. Helen's horn-rimmed glasses framed dark blue eyes that seemed to dance with delight.

Maris smiled at the tall, elderly woman. "It's a bit on the crazy side."

Helen grinned as she nodded. "Have you ever been to one of these?"

Maris shook her head. "It was after my time." She glanced at the poster in the window of the market, the same one she had on display at the B&B. "The Fifth Annual Blues on the Bay Music Festival." Though she'd visited her aunt as a youngster, her adult work had taken her far away. It'd been years since she'd been back. She regarded Helen. "Are you a blues fan?"

"Oh, definitely," Helen said. As the elderly woman gazed at the plaza, Maris noted the large canvas tote bag she carried. Her latest doily projects were likely inside. "I mean, even if you weren't, how could you not like this?" Helen peered at her. "Are you?"

Maris smirked a little. "Only by association. Aunt Glenda was the real fan."

In the parlor at the B&B, an old Victrola was accompanied by Glenda's vast collection of blues albums. Her aunt had played them for her while they'd amused themselves with board and card games or dabbled with the Ouija board.

"Your aunt was instrumental in getting the festival started," Helen said.

Maris stared at her. "I didn't know that."

She turned back to the plaza, where a sound system was being installed in the red Oriental gazebo, and a second stage was being built at the far end. Large tents sheltered booths where food and drinks would be sold, as well as t-shirts, trinkets, and music. There were even tables where the musicians would sign autographs. It was a massive undertaking—one for which she had a new appreciation.

Helen nodded her gray head. "Yes, she was quite the driving force, your aunt."

Maris had to smile at the thought. "She was that." It was actually a trait they shared.

Helen glanced at the crochet club. "Millicent is on the festival committee, so naturally we've been privy to some of the goings on." When she turned her gaze back to Maris, she arched her eyebrows. "Perhaps next year we can look to the younger generation for some organizational help. Maybe even, shall we say, carry on a family tradition."

Maris knew a buttonhole when she heard one, but the fact that Glenda had been involved with the start of the festival really did put it in a new light. Of course she had her hands full at the B&B during the festivities, but perhaps in the weeks leading up to it, she could find time to help.

"Who is the committee head?" Maris inquired.

Helen grinned at her. "A new one is elected every year. You just have to put your hat in the ring. This year it was Aurora Puddlefoot." She nodded to herself. "Marvelous with management."

Maris thought back to visiting the proprietor of the largest store on the plaza. Three stories tall, with everything from souvenirs to clothing and furniture, Magical Finds had at least a dozen employees.

"Yes," Maris said, "I could see that."

"Well," the older woman said, "I won't delay you any longer." She turned to go, but paused. "Unless, of course, you were stopping in for some crocheting."

"Unfortunately not," Maris said. She indicated the market as she repositioned the purse on her shoulder. "I've got a bit of shopping to do."

"Yes," Helen said, nodding. "I'm sure we're all quite busy right now." A smile lit up her face. "Good day to you."

"Have a good one," Maris replied.

• • • • •

The market was busier than usual too. Shoppers, mostly tourists, were everywhere. As she took her cart up and down the aisles, Maris even noticed that Howard had hired on some new help. Young people were busily stocking shelves and answering questions from the customers. But luckily, by the time she was finished gathering everything that the B&B needed, the front counter was empty and the retired physics professor and owner of the market waved her over.

"Good morning, Maris," he said, his smile lifting his white mustache and deepening the crow's feet at the corners of his dark eyes. Though he still bore an uncanny resemblance to Einstein, his hair was neatly brushed today and his mustache combed and trimmed.

"Good morning, Howard," she said, as she unloaded the boxed goods first. "I've never seen the store so busy."

"I have," he said, quickly ringing up the goods. He gave her a wink. "This time last year."

Maris chuckled. "Well, I can see that you're prepared." One of the new employees rolled a bucket and mop past them. "The extra help is a great idea."

As Howard bagged the groceries, he said, "It's a necessity." He indicated her basket as she unloaded the vegetables. "The B&B must be full."

"Absolutely," she said. "This week's been booked for months. At first I had no idea what was going on." She laughed a little. "I told Cookie it must be a new holiday that I don't know about. She clued me in. In a way, a new holidays exactly what it seems like."

Suddenly she remembered the one item she hadn't found. "Oh, I almost forgot. I couldn't find any scrub sponges. Are you out?"

He was putting a loaded bag into the cart, but paused to look at her. "No scrubbies?" He set the bag down, and held up one finger. "Let me just check in the back." He zipped over to the door behind the counter, and disappeared.

As soon as it closed, Maris heard the usual sounds of rummaging that accompanied one of her requests. At first it sounded like boxes dragging along the ground. But then there was a bump, as though something had fallen against the door. Grunting then ensued, along with more scraping sounds and a few more bumps. But Maris didn't worry. Not only was this the time-honored process, but Howard always came up with the goods, no matter how obscure. She bagged the rest of the groceries and put everything in the cart.

But when Howard finally emerged, Maris had to stare at him in surprise. Not only was his hair going in every direction, he was sweating and breathing hard. His shocked expression and empty hands said it all.

"It's missing," he gasped. "It's gone."

Maris cocked her head at him. "The scrub sponges?" To say she was shocked was an understatement. He'd never let her down. But he obviously had a lot to deal with and she didn't want to add to the pressure. She held up a hand. "No problem. They're not a–"

"No," he whispered harshly, stumbling back to her, "not the scrubbies." He put both hands on the counter and leaned forward. "My crystal ball."

• • • • •

Buy The Witch Who Heard the Music

FREE BOOK

If you'd like to learn how Maris arrived in Pixie Point Bay and got her start, you can read *The Witch Who Saw the Light* for FREE by signing up for my newsletter at the link below.

Get A Free Book

DEDICATION

For Mr. Bee's Knees

COPYRIGHT

Copyright © 2020 Emma Belmont

This is a work of fiction. Names, characters, places, and incidents are products of the author's imagination or are used fictitiously and are not to be construed as real. Any resemblance to actual events, locales, organizations, or persons, living or dead, is coincidental.

All rights reserved. No part of this book may be used or reproduced in any manner, stored in or introduced into a retrieval system, or transmitted, in any form, or by any means (electronic, mechanical, photocopying, recording, or otherwise), without the prior written consent of the copyright owner.

The scanning, uploading, and distribu-

www.ingramcontent.com/pod-product-compliance
Lightning Source LLC
Chambersburg PA
CBHW070936190726
48292CB00004B/1198